DEADLY ADVERSARIES

DEBRA PARMLEY

Belo Dia
PUBLISHING INC

CHAPTER 1

Texas 1881

$\mathscr{T}$exas Ranger Jacob Brace watched as his best friend, Matthew Truman, read the letter from his sister, his pleasant expression erased by a deep frown as he read fast, before crumpling the letter in his fist. Matt threw the letter on the ground and then hurried toward the stables without glancing at Jake or saying a word.

Jake picked up the letter, smoothed it out, and read Carolyn's perfect delicate penmanship.

November 30, 1881

Dear Matt,

I wasn't sure how to reach you fast. You always say not to spend the money on a telegram since you're often nowhere near a town. So I'm sending this to the ranger office and marking it urgent, in hopes they find a way to get this to you as soon as possible.

I wish I wasn't writing this. Father is gone. He was out

moving the cattle from the summer pastures to the winter pastures and someone shot him. They murdered him and no one knows who did it. Mother isn't doing so well and I'm scared. Mr. Henning Holland says father lost the ranch in a card game. But I don't believe him. You know what father used to say about gambling. But there's a paper he signed that gives Mr. Holland the ranch and we have to move out one week after the funeral unless I become Mrs. Henning Holland. I can't stand him and won't marry him. Come home, Matt. We need you.

Love,

Carolyn.

Jake shook his head.

Damn. This letter is three days old already and Denman Springs is a two-day ride from here.

Jake stuffed the letter into his pocket and followed Matt into the stables.

"I'm going with you," Jake said.

"It's my problem. I'll take care of it," Matt muttered, his mood as dark as Jake had ever seen it. Understandably so. Matt could be especially fierce if women or children were being harmed. Then he'd see red and would not let up or listen to anyone, other than Jake.

"Okay." Jake started gathering his own gear and preparing to ride. "You take care of it." He nodded at Matt who was barely looking at him, preoccupied with his own thoughts and preparations. "I'm riding with you. Got nothing else better to do right now."

They had just finishing tracking two men and seeing that justice was served. But they were used to riding out again soon after they finished a job. There was always another job to do. This time though, it was personal.

It didn't need to be said that Jake would go with Matt.

They were as close as brothers and had worked together since they'd joined the ranger troupe.

Matt would need Jake's cooler head to find the murderer and protect his sister. He was going along whether Matt wanted him to or not.

Matt hurried to pack his gear and Jake matched the pace Matt set. Soon they both were riding for Nightingale Ranch. As they worked together and were seldom apart, they fell into a natural rhythm, this time a harder faster rhythm than usual.

Whoever had killed Matthew Truman's father had no idea that two of the deadliest men in Texas had now made it their business to hunt him down. And Carolyn Truman wasn't marrying any man she didn't want to marry. If Matt couldn't stop the wedding and Carolyn had been coerced into it and didn't want to remain married, Matt would have no hesitation at making sure Carolyn was widowed. He didn't tolerate mistreating women or children.

Jake would not want to be Mr. Henning Holland right now.

"AT LEAST BE nice to Mr. Holland." Sally Truman said to Carolyn. "He's done nothing to you, yet you act as if he has a disease you could catch." She paced in her bedroom, where she spent most of her time lately crying.

"He gives me dis-ease, that is for certain," Carolyn said as she watched her mother pace.

"And you have always made that quite clear," her mother replied. "When a man is in love with you, it is unkind to treat him the way you have been. I raised you to be kinder than that."

"He will take any kindness as encouragement." She shook her head. "I can't afford to be nice to him."

"If you would just consider his proposal." Her mother sat on the bed, as if tired now. "You would be well settled and never have to worry about losing your home like I did." Her mother began to cry softly again.

But Carolyn couldn't let her mother's tears sway her. "I would never be settled married to that man. I'd be on edge constantly."

"At least think about it."

Carolyn nodded to appease her mother long enough to stop this topic of conversation. She hung the black mourning dress her mother would wear to the funeral over the pink velvet covered seat in the corner and prepared to leave the room

"Mind what I said now," Sally Truman said to Carolyn's retreating back as she left.

"Yes, mama." Carolyn walked from the room and then stopped to lean back against the wall in the hallway, exhausted down to her bones. Exhausted with all of it. She closed her eyes.

So tired. She exhaled a long slow breath.

Sally had been distraught and spent much time in her room crying after learning that her husband, Robert Truman, had been shot. Leaving things up to Carolyn. Neither of them had been prepared for the shock and the grief, which washed over them.

Preparation for the funeral and attending to her mother had taken every bit of Carolyn's time and every ounce of energy. She'd stayed too busy to grieve beyond that first night when she'd hurried to write a letter to her brother while she sat at the desk in the parlor, crying.

Now, minding what her mother had said, she ran the words through her mind again.

Be nice to Mr. Henning Holland. At least consider his marriage proposal.

But she couldn't. She'd never been able to smile for the man, even when she was little. Now he wanted to marry her? She couldn't possibly. He made her stomach turn. She grew uncomfortable the minute he walked into a room.

How other people can stand to be around him, even welcome his company I'll never know.

She'd told her mother often enough as she was growing up, that Mr. Henning Holland made her uncomfortable, but her mother always brushed it off. He had nice manners, was wealthy and had a big ranch, right next to theirs. So Carolyn had seen him often as she was growing up. Too often.

Big questions now rose in Carolyn's mind again.

He has plenty of money. Why does he want our much smaller ranch? Why does he want me?

She had no answers. And maybe it didn't matter what the answers were. Because knowing the answers was unlikely to change thing Mr. Holland was insisting upon.

Robert Truman had maintained the ranch Aunt Doe left them, building it up as best he could, but this year it had become even more difficult. Now he was gone.

Mother and I need help.

They might lose the ranch even without the problem of Mr. Henning Holland.

Carolyn had tried, but she couldn't round up all the cattle and bring them in. They'd scattered when her pa was shot. She wouldn't be surprised if some of them had gone missing, or were mixed in with the cattle on Mr. Henning Holland's ranch, though he'd told her they hadn't seen any extra cattle, which didn't belong to him. His cowhands swore by it.

We need those cattle back, Carolyn thought as she leaned against the wall squeezing her eyes closed tight.

"Oh Matthew, come soon," she whispered. "There isn't much time." She sent up a prayer that God would speed him home to them. It would take a miracle. The funeral was tomorrow.

THE DAY OF THE FUNERAL, people kept arriving with food, which was a good thing, as she and her mama hadn't fixed enough fried chicken to feed them all. They'd cooked every chicken they had except for three laying hens and they couldn't cook them or they'd have no eggs.

Carolyn hadn't realized so many people knew her Pa, but here they were from two towns nearby, Homer and Nacogdoches, bringing food and paying their respects to him.

The kitchen groaned with the weight of all that food. Homemade dumplings, potato salad, beans and rice, sausages, cornbread, biscuits, jellies and pies. Yet none of it looked good to her, as in her grief she'd completely lost her appetite. She kept hoping Matt would arrive before the funeral, but he hadn't.

The homemade wooden coffin, built by a Mr. Gant, the furniture maker in Homer, stood on two sawhorses in the parlor. Mr. Gant was also acting as the funeral director, and the preacher, Seth Mills, would be preaching the sermon.

Though the food didn't comfort Carolyn, all the stories about her Pa did. She was hearing things she hadn't known about him, along with things she had. The stories everyone was sharing brought his memory closer for all of them. It seemed he'd helped plenty of people and he'd done it in a quiet way, few but the ones he'd helped had known about, which was why Carolyn and her mother had never heard the stories before. She hated that Matt was missing all this and longed for the loving support of her older brother.

After several hours, when it seemed everyone had arrived and had eaten, they all gathered in the parlor and in the hallway, listening as pastor Mills read the service and preached a sermon.

Carolyn sat holding her mother's hand, trying to be strong for her. She had to be strong.

No one else is here to do it. Where is Matthew?

She hadn't heard back from him after sending the letter, and he hadn't arrived in time for the funeral.

She felt the heat of Mr. Henning Holland's gaze upon her back without turning her head and she tried to ignore him. It seemed he was always watching her. She'd been trying to ignore him since he'd arrived.

Sally Truman went up to the casket and placed a single rose from her garden upon Robert Truman's chest. "You were the best husband I had and the best father to my children. I love you with all of my heart and always will, until my dying day. Then we will be together again." Taking an embroidered hanky, she covered her face to dab at her tears and pastor Mills helped her move to the side to wait for Carolyn.

Carolyn stepped up and placed her rose on her stepfather's chest, next to her mother's rose. "You loved me like your own, until I was your own, and I know if Matthew were here, he'd say the same. I love you Pa." Her voice broke on the last word as she started to cry. A thing she had sworn to herself she would not do. Not with Mr. Henning Holland watching and seeing her weakness.

He would use any excuse to touch her, and him offering her comfort in front of the others where she couldn't jerk away was the last thing she wanted. Forcing her tears back, she straightened her spine, showing everyone how strong she was. She would not break down in front of them.

The casket was closed and the four pallbearers carried the casket out to load it onto the wagon, which would carry Robert Truman to his final resting place in the cemetery.

Mourners rode along behind the wagon until everyone had reached the cemetery. Four men then carried and lowered the pine wood box, which held the remains of Robert Truman, into the east Texas soil as the women cried into their handkerchiefs. Then pastor Miller spoke the final prayers for the dead and Sally Truman started crying loudly as the other women began to wail.

Carolyn couldn't stand the way wailing took place at funerals, the way people would "take on" or the way they judged anyone who did not "take on", questioning whether they cared as much. Judgmental eyes watched her, as she stood silent, holding her tears back, and not wailing with the others.

Setting her jaw, she refused to wail or to break down in front of them.

After her pa was lowered into the ground a line of mourners formed to say their final thoughts and goodbyes before everyone left. She refused to look at Mr. Henning Holland though she knew exactly where he stood in the line. Soon he stood right in front of them with his hat in his hand.

He reached for her mother's hand with his free hand and then stood holding it. "Mrs. Truman," he said. "You have my sincerest condolences. I know your loss is great. Robert Truman was a good man. A family man. If there's anything I can do for you, let me know."

"Thank you, that is very kind of you," her mother said softly. "There's nothing." She shook her head as her soft voice faded.

Mr. Henning Holland sounded so sincere but Carolyn felt deep down in her gut that he wasn't. Her mother was being taken in by his nice manners, as usual.

Sally Truman, despite the difficulties of her past, still had a tendency to trust people until they proved that she shouldn't have. Rob had always dealt with others in their community, leaving Sally to simply be the sweet woman she was. Sally shared her good cooking and her sweet smiles with everyone and everyone loved her.

When Mr. Henning Holland stopped in front of Caroline next, she faced him directly and said, "If you really meant what you said, there is one thing you can do, which would ease our suffering greatly."

"Of course," he said. "Anything for you, my dear."

"You can tear up that promissory note."

He sent her a large smile while his eyes bored into hers making her stomach uneasy.

"I will give it to you," His eyes lit as if from a fire within. "As a wedding gift, the morning after our wedding, if you wish. That is my promise. You have but to say yes."

"In which case the ranch would still be yours by way of marriage." She shook her head. "That is no gift."

"Ah, but then you and your mother would be taken care of, quite well I might add."

"No," she said with another more vehement shake of her head.

"This isn't the time or the place for an argument," her mother shushed her.

She pursed her lips, which Mr. Holland's gaze centered upon before he turned to her mother again. "My apologizes. I was swept away by your daughter's beauty once again and forgot my manners. She has that affect on me. Quite a distraction. Again, my condolences."

Carolyn watched his retreating back with narrowed eyes as the next neighbors moved through the line to speak to them.

On the way back to the ranch house, her mother began to cry again as Carolyn drove their wagon. "It's too much losing Rob and now we'll lose our home in just one week. Where will we go? I lost my home once. I can't go through that again," She sobbed into her handkerchief. "Sweetheart, you don't know what it was like. You were too little to understand. You don't understand now. If you'd just consider marrying Mr. Henning Holland, we wouldn't have to move."

Carolyn's hands tightened on the reigns. "You're wrong. I do remember things. Sunflowers and fields. I remember papa shouting. A lot. I hid under the covers, because he was so loud and I was afraid of him. But that's all I remember of your first husband, all I knew of my father. To me, Rob was always our pa. I don't want us to lose the ranch either, and you know I love you mama, but I can't marry that man. You know what it's like to be married to the wrong man. Is that really what you want for me?"

Sally's brow furrowed at the words.

Carolyn shook her head. "There has to be another way. Matthew will come back to help us, you'll see."

Murmurs at the funeral had moved around Sally, just out of reach of her hearing, as none would have been unkind to her face, but Carolyn was aware of the murmurs and watching the gossips.

That tall Mrs. Brown, who couldn't help but talk about everyone, pointing out flaws she perceived in everyone else, apparently couldn't hold her tongue even at a funeral.

"Her boy rode off and left them, you know. He's been gone for years, Injuns killed him. Now his mother has no one. They'll never be able to keep that ranch now that Rob is gone. One of them will have to marry."

Anger filled Carolyn with each word she overheard and she wanted to retort.

Matthew rode away yes, but it was to join the Texas Rangers. And he's only been gone two years.

Matt was alive and he would come the minute he heard, but deep down Carolyn worried he wouldn't receive the letter in time to stop this nightmare from unfolding even further.

None were bold enough to speak gossip directly to her, or her mother, but instead they spoke off to the side where they thought the women wouldn't hear. Carolyn's hearing being far keener than any of them realized, had heard every gossiping word.

The nasty gossips. Couldn't they hold their tongues at a funeral?

Carolyn didn't give two hoots for the women with their fine society manners and their nasty gossiping tongues.

They'll see when Matt comes riding back into town wearing his badge. Then they'll all see.

She hoped and prayed he would come soon.

UNROLLING HIS BEDROLL, Jake said, "Tell me more about your home. I know the ranch is five hundred acres and your pa was running cattle."

They'd stopped to rest their horses, who could only be pushed so far. The men would catch some sleep as well before pressing on. Though he was in a hurry, Matt said, "I ain't gonna be like no Injun, riding my horse til it dies and then taking another man's horse to replace it."

"I agree. You set the pace, I'm just here to cover your back," Jake said.

Matt despised Injuns, as the ones he'd met were dangerous men who stole and killed. Matt despised Mexicans for the same reason. Jake could understand where Matt was coming from, even though he'd met Indians who weren't killing, stealing outlaws and there were peaceable Mexicans as well. Jake's take on it was, men were like dogs. Some were good, but the rabid ones had to be taken down. Which was where the Rangers came in. Doing the things other men either wouldn't or couldn't do.

Matt pulled off his boots and slipped into his bedroll before continuing. Once settled, he started talking again. "Much of the land is heavy with timber, so he can't run cattle on all five hundred acres. He's always done everything himself so he sticks to running small herds."

Jake noted that Matt was still speaking of his father in the present tense, as if it hadn't settled in just yet that his father was gone.

"This year has been bad, according to Carolyn. Nothing I could do about that. Even if I'd stayed home. Pa and me used to fight about that. He wanted me to stay. I couldn't. Now it's too late."

Jake knew Matt would be feeling bad about that, even as

he heard it in his voice. Knowing Matt, he'd do everything he could to make up for it.

"Did you and your pa get along, other than disagreeing about you staying on the ranch?"

"We got along great, other than that one sticking point."

Jake nodded. "Wish I could've met him."

"I do too." Matt wadded up the padding that would make his pillow, punching it twice. "I'm no rancher." He lay back and crossed his arms behind his head, looking up at the stars. "Nothing I can do about making that ranch successful, but if mama and Carolyn want to stay, I'll figure out a way to see it happens."

"What's your mama like?"

"She's a smallish woman with gray hair and a quiet smile. Appears soft, but she's stronger than she lets on. She saved my life in a gunfight."

"That's a story you never told me. How did she do that?"

Matt smiled, still looking up at the sky. "She shot my pa. Her first husband."

"Is that right?"

"That's right. He was running with outlaws. Took me with him. I was seven. I learned how to play poker and how to deal. After mama shot him, Robert Truman became my pa. He played poker with me once and then said, "Matthew, if you really want to play, I'll play with you. I don't want you running around somewhere else playing. But I think out of respect for your mother, I would prefer not to play. Think it over and then decide if you still want to play."

"What did you decide?"

"I didn't play when I was on the ranch. Still don't. Out of respect for mama. Only play when I'm away."

"So you don't believe your pa lost the ranch in a poker game."

"He wouldn't have signed the ranch away even with a gun to his head. I know he didn't lose it in a damn card game. Henning Holland is pulling something. I have to find out what happened to pa and find out how Holland got a hold of that note."

"What about your sister?"

"What about her?"

"Tell me more about her."

"Carolyn is like sunshine. Almost always smiling, cheerful, chatty and doesn't sit still for long. Her smile can light up the whole room."

"Sounds like the opposite of you, ya moody varmint."

Matt laughed. A sound good to Jake's ears. "She is."

"I can't wait to meet her."

Matt looked over at Jake, quiet, thinking about something.

Jake wondered what it was.

"She knows how to ride and how to shoot," Matt said. "Pa and me taught her. But she'd rather sew or dance."

"Is she a good cook?"

"Her cooking isn't as good as mama's, but it's good."

"She's four years younger than you. I'm surprised she's not married already."

"Says she'll only marry for love and she's in no hurry."

"This Henning Holland. What's he like?"

"Wealthy businessman. Has a big ranch, right next to ours. Pa has around five hundred acres, but Mr. Holland probably has a thousand acres or more by now. Doesn't get his hands dirty. Leaves it all to the ranch hands. He's had his eye on Carolyn for a long time, but she's always disliked him. He offered to marry her as soon as she turned of age. Approached pa. She wasn't interested in marrying anyone yet. Mama told pa she didn't believe in arranged marriages and she wanted Caroline to enjoy her childhood as long as she could. When Carolyn did reach the point where she'd consider marrying, she announced to everyone that she would only marry for love."

"She's a romantic."

Matthew frowned. "Yes, I suppose she is. She likes to dance, reads the Bible and poetry. Pa wouldn't let her go to barn dances without him, because she needs a better chaperone than mother. Mother thinks the best of everyone and sometimes she's wrong. Pretty words swayed Caroline's head a few times when she was younger and pa had to step in. He always says she's a younger image of mama and it is up to us to protect them both. "

"What's your mama look like?"

"She's gone grey now, but she used to have strawberry blonde hair. Like Carolyn. Everyone says you can tell she and I are brother and sister because of our eyes."

Jake imagined a picture in his mind of what Carolyn looked like.

So Carolyn had those inquisitive green eyes that Matt had. Intelligent eyes that communicated much and had saved them both many times in a fight when Matt had sent a quick glance to Jake which he immediately read.

Jake had an image in his mind now of what Matt's sister must be like and what she must look like. An innocent. Beautiful or at least pretty, if men kept coming around for her.

It was a good thing they were riding to the ranch to make sure the women were safe and nothing else bad happened. Having their pa shot was bad enough.

Though Jake kept this part of himself quiet if not hidden, truth was he was a bit of a romantic himself.

There was nothing wrong with marrying for love. In fact, it was one of the best reasons.

Thing was, he hadn't found love yet either. Plenty of lust but none of the women were ones he'd want to spend his life with. He wasn't ready to settle down. His parents were content on their horse farm and with their other two sons, they didn't really need him there, Jake had been itchy to travel, to see new things and to have adventures. Stopping bad men from harming good people appealed to him, especially after learning the truth of what had happened to his mother, over some gold, before his mother and father met. Men's greed over gold had damn near killed her.

The reputation of the Texas rangers had him riding for Texas, once he was of an age and had a good horse and the means to outfit himself and get there. Then he'd met Matt who'd also gone to the ranger station to sign up and they'd been best friends ever since.

"She's got a border collie," Matt said, interrupting Jake's thoughts. "Named Dash. If he likes you, you're golden in Carolyn's eyes. Dash is the best judge of character I know."

"Border collies are highly intelligent," Jake said.

"Yes, they are."

"I had one as a boy. Bandit. Best friend I ever had."

Matt grunted.

Not sure what that grunt meant, Jake added. "Before I met you."

"Thanks. Well, you'll meet my family soon enough."

"Looking forward to it," Jake said, feeling awkward now that he'd let his softer side out. A side rangers rarely showed. "We'd best get to sleep. Unless you want to talk some more about your pa."

"I'm good. Need sleep. Night."

"Night."

The next morning they were up before sunrise, wasting no time with breakfast or even coffee. Jake pulled out a piece of beef jerky to chew on for his breakfast as he packed his things back on his horse. This time he was the quiet one, as they prepared to ride out. The image Matt had painted of Carolyn was on his mind. She was an innocent, like his mother had been, before his father had rescued her. One reason Jake had joined the rangers was to protect the innocent and this was on his mind as he prepared to ride.

CHAPTER 2

Two riders approached the ranch house at a fast pace. Carolyn stepped out onto the porch, watching them ride in. Dread filled her as she waited.

Lately riders brought only bad news and she didn't know these men.

What did they want? Mr. Henning Holland could have sent them, or they could be outlaws.

As the men neared, her anxiety soared.

These men were tall, longhaired and full bearded. Each rode a big black horse and each wore buckskins. Armed, with crisscross bandoliers heavy with bullets, two pistols on each side, and long guns sticking up from their rifle holsters, where they could pull the guns out fast, they were ready for trouble, or they'd cause trouble. Their wild and dangerous appearance as they rode nearer caused her to reach inside the front door for the shotgun she kept there in case of trouble.

She would be far outgunned if they brought a fight, but she'd do her best and if they meant to harm her, she might shoot at least one of them before they shot her, if she were ready to shoot first.

Ratcheting the shotgun back, she raised it to her shoulder and waited, ready to shoot.

They didn't so much as slow at the sight of her. That fact alarmed her even more as they kept on coming toward her, fast.

Aiming, she fired one shot over their heads and then yelled. "Stop right there."

They just kept coming.

Laughter was the response of the man on her left, as he rode closer. "Haw, haw, haw," he guffawed. "Your aim ain't improved much."

That voice. Could it be?

Carolyn tipped her head, frowning and squinting to see the man with the big familiar laugh. The other man sat on his horse grinning. Both appeared to find her amusing and kept their expressions and body language relaxed and friendly.

Dash, her border collie, ran from the barn to the laughing man and horse, barking.

"Hello boy," the laughing man said.

Suddenly Dash stopped, wagged his tail and looked happily up at the man. Then he gave a happy yip, followed by another.

The man looked down at the dog. "I missed you too, Dash." He glanced back to Carolyn. "There's gray in his muzzle now," he said.

"Matt?" she asked, not lowering the gun, trying to make sure. He sounded like Matt, he knew the dog's name, but he didn't look like Matt.

"Yeah," he laughed. "Don't put no holes in me, or my friend Jake here."

She lowered the gun, but still wary said, "What did mama bring all the way from Kansas for me?" No one else but mama and her brother would know the answer.

"Sunflower seeds," he answered. "Now put that gun away before you shoot your foot off." He laughed again.

This time Jake was laughing with him, his intense dark eyes taking her in.

She'd nearly shot her foot the year she was learning to shoot. Matt and pa had promised not to tell mama.

Caroline leaned the gun against the porch post and then ran down the steps and went racing toward him. "Matt, I'm so glad you're here!"

As she got closer to the men, she stopped and wrinkled her nose. "What did you get into? You stink."

"Well, hello to you too, little sister." Matt got down off his horse and took the reins in one hand.

She laughed, happy to have him home again, even if he did stink.

"Rode straight here after I got your letter. Guess we are kind of ripe," Mat said. He shrugged over his shoulder. "This here is Jacob Brace, my best friend and fellow ranger."

"Ma'am," Jacob's deep voice reached inside of her, awakening a resonation, as he tipped his hat and nodded at her, his dark eyes intense beneath the hat, which shadowed his eyes. "Nice to meet you. You can call me Jake."

Oh gracious, she thought. *That voice. Too bad he's so stinky and rough looking and not more handsome.*

"Nice to meet you, Jake." She watched him dismount.

Lord he's a big man.

He was at least six foot tall, towering over her smaller five foot six inch frame, his shoulders broad, and his thighs thick with muscle beneath buckskins as he climbed down from the horse. He was the largest, most intimidating man she had ever seen.

She took a step backward instead of forward, her eyes widening.

Both men wore many guns, as well as carried big knives and, was that a bloodstain on the leg of Jake's pants?

Men didn't wash buckskins and these must've seen a lot of fighting or hunting. Her nose crinkled up at the scent of them.

No wonder they both smelled bad.

"What, no hug for your brother?" Matt opened his arms. "You gonna let a little stink get between us? I haven't seen you for two years. You look mighty nice, Carolyn."

She stepped nearer and gave him a hug while holding her breath, though he nearly squeezed the breath out of her with his tight, fierce hug. His arms and hard chest were much stronger than she remembered.

"Rangering has toughened you up," she said, when he'd let loose of her, and she could breathe again. "I've missed you."

"It has." He agreed. "And I've missed you. I always said, I have the prettiest little sister in all of Texas, but now look at you, all grown up since I been gone and prettier than ever."

She blushed beneath the compliment and Jake's watchful, appreciative gaze. "Thank you," she murmured.

Matt looked past her toward the house. "Where's mama?"

"I'll tell her you're here," she said. "She'll be so happy."

"Naw, I'll go see her now, and surprise her, and then we'll clean up. Need to put the horses up first though."

"I can do that," Jake said. "Go on and see your ma."

Matt nodded. "Thanks. Barns that way." He pointed and

then handed the reins of his horse to Jake and Jake headed for the barn leading the horses.

Briefly Carolyn watched the big man go.

"He grew up on a horse farm and is real good with them," Matt said. "If you need anything else done, while he's here, tell me."

"They need fed."

Matt nodded. "Hey Jake?"

Jake paused, turning to glance at them.

"Feed the other horses for me?"

"Sure."

"Thanks."

Jake gave a nod and turned back.

Matt and Carolyn headed for the house.

"Aren't you going to shave and clean up before you see mama?" she asked.

"No." He shook his head. "I don't want anyone else to recognize me or know that I'm back in town while I'm hunting for pa's killer."

"Oh, I see. Well, I hardly recognized you until you spoke."

"And you still weren't sure."

A small hope rose in her chest. Maybe now that Matt was back, he'd find the man who'd shot their pa, while also stopping Mr. Henning Holland from taking the ranch. It was asking a lot and there wasn't much time. But Matt was a Texas Ranger now. If anyone could do this, Matt could. He was a fearsome sight. And he'd probably scare mama half to death. She'd best speak her mind before that happened.

"I'll take you to her, but you're a fearsome sight, Matthew." Carolyn frowned. "And you stink. Don't sit on the bed, as I'd have a time getting the covers from her to wash them."

"What's wrong with ma?" he asked, astutely realizing something was.

"She stays in her bedroom a lot, cries and says she can't lose another home. She seems to want everything to stay the same. Everything in the room is just as pa left it. I wouldn't dare touch a thing. It sets her off if I even pick up one of pa's things. She says she's not leaving this ranch til they carry her dead body out. I don't like her talking about death, Matt. It worries me. I'm afraid she'll miss pa so much, she'll want to join him."

"I'll talk to her," Matthew said.

"I'm scared. What's going to happen to us? To the ranch? This is our home!"

"One thing at a time," he reassured her. "Nobody is taking this ranch and mama doesn't have to leave it if she don't want to."

"I'm so glad you're here." She placed her hand on his arm and he wrapped his arm around her and gave her a firm squeeze. She ignored his stink as best she could.

Inside the ranch house, Matt took in his surroundings as they walked toward their mother's room. The ranch had fallen on hard times, and it was evident in the way their home had been taken care of, or rather neglected. Suddenly he stopped. "Let me see your hands," he said.

"Why?" Carolyn held them out to him.

He turned them over, seeing the red roughness and blisters. "Have you had any help here, or have you been doing everything yourself?" he asked in a quiet, low voice.

"Just me. We don't have the money to hire anyone."

"I'm home now. You don't have do everything yourself any more," he said said in a firm voice, dropping her hands.

She struggled with what to say as he dropped her hands. Their pa had struggled with the ranch for the last two years, since Matthew went away. It had been a source of contention between the two men and she didn't want it to become one with her and her brother. Matt had said he wasn't cut out for ranching and staying in one place, but Robert Truman had never understood why his stepson couldn't put the past in the past and stay home to help them. He often reminded Matt the ranch would belong to him and Carolyn one day. Now it appeared it would belong to neither of them. And right now, she did need help.

"I, I haven't been able to gather all the cattle," Caroline said. "They're still out in the summer pasture but there's broken fences and I think some of the cattle are missing. I couldn't bring them in or find the missing ones. And I tried to fix the fences, but mama needed me. And I didn't have any help."

"You take care of mama. Jake and me will bring the cattle in and mend the fences. Do whatever needs to be done. You stay home until things settle down some and we know it's safe again."

"Thank you, Matt."

"Carolyn, who are you talking to?"

Their mother's wavering voice came from her bedroom, the wavering in her voice a sure sign that she was crying and Carolyn glanced at Matt, wondering what to say.

He won't be prepared for this. The sound of mama's crying. He never could stand hearing her cry. And she's thinner.

"Prepare yourself, Matt. She's lost a lot of weight."

He squared his shoulders, took a deep breath and then walked into the room. "Hello, mama. I rode hard for home, just as soon as I heard."

"Matthew, is that really you?" Sally Truman sat on the bed, shock across her face.

He took off his hat, as if belatedly remembering his manners. "Yes, mama. It's me."

"Why, I hardly know you, beneath your beard and mustache."

"I came straight here to see you. I've missed you." He approached her and twisted his hat in his hands. "I hate what happened to pa and what it's done to you." He took her hand and held it in his. "We're not losing this ranch." He squeezed her hand. "You're not going anywhere. I'm here now. I'm gonna find pa's killer and bring justice."

Her eyes filled with tears. "It won't bring him back."

"No it won't."

"I miss him so."

"I miss him too."

"Don't you go getting yourself killed, Matthew Wheeler. I can't lose you too."

Carolyn's eyes widened at the use of Matthew's birth name.

His back tensed, hearing it.

He'd legally been Matthew Truman since he was eight and Sally's new husband had adopted them. The slip of the tongue was unusual for their mother and showed how distraught she was.

"Men have tried. They always fail."

Matt's tone of voice made Carolyn believe, but Sally's eyes gazed into Matthew's as if searching for something.

Silence stretched.

Finally Sally spoke. "Well. You'd best have a bath or they'll smell you coming."

"That's my spirited mother. Rob always said you had starch in your skirts."

She smiled for the first time since her husband had passed. "That he did." She nodded.

25

Relief filled Sally.

Things would be better now that Matt was home.

They already were. Though what they'd do about Mr. Henning Holland she did not know.

"I'd best set up your bath," Sally said.

"We'll help." He said.

"I'll see you after you've cleaned up. Take your time," Sally said. "You could use a real good soaking."

"Yes, ma'am."

Sally smiled at both her children as they left the room.

MATTHEW AND JAKE carried the long metal tub into the kitchen.

"Where do you want it?" Jake asked.

"Near the fireplace," Carolyn said.

"Do you need more wood chopped?" Jake asked, eying the dwindling stack.

"Yes," Carolyn looked at the stack and sighed. "I haven't been able to keep up."

"There's a bin out back," Matt said. "Check there first. Pa kept it filled."

"It's very low," Carolyn said.

"I'll check it," Jake said as he moved toward the back door. They watched him go out.

"What are your thoughts on moving into town? Do you want to stay now that pa's gone?"

"Mama won't leave this place," she said, and then she looked over at Jake who came in.

"Found enough wood for tonight," Jake said. "I'll chop more in the morning."

She nodded and looked back at Matt. "So it doesn't matter what my thoughts are."

"Your thoughts always matter," Jake said.

He didn't know what they were discussing, but she needed to know that her thoughts mattered and it was okay to speak up. Some women needed to be encouraged in the way that his father encouraged his mother.

"Jake's right." Matt stoked the fire. "Your thoughts do matter."

Carolyn started boiling water. "It's gotten harder to live here. Ranching is hard work."

"That it is," Jake said. "My parents raise horses."

"And yet you came to Texas to be a ranger, like Matt." Carolyn smiled.

"Yes, ma'am." Jake nodded.

"No need to ma'am me, I'm just Carolyn."

"Carolyn, like Matt, I'm an older brother. But unlike Matt, both my siblings are boys."

"So your father has plenty of help."

"He does. But he also runs smaller herds. Doesn't take on more than he can handle."

"Why did you join the Texas rangers? I know why Matt joined."

"I wanted to right wrongs and to see more of this great land."

"And have you done that?"

"Yes, I have done both." He nodded.

The men began to bring in water to fill the tub and talking ceased.

Taking a bath, like everything on the ranch, required work.

Carolyn carried in soap and drying cloths, a comb and

scissors, implying they needed to trim their hair and beards. "Here you go," she said, placing the things on the table.

"Thank you," Jake said. "Bath is gonna feel real good." He rubbed his hand over his beard. "Been a while."

"Take all the time you need. I'll be in the parlor reading."

Then she left them to it and went into the parlor where she would wait. Dash padded along beside her. The last place he would want to be was in the kitchen during bath time.

She sat on the rocker in the parlor. Dash put his head on her lap.

"Hello boy." She looked into his loving eyes. "Sure you don't want to stay in the kitchen with the men while they have a bath?"

At the word bath, Dash pulled away and hung his head. He did not like to have a bath. Carolyn giggled and felt her spirits lifting for the first time in a long time.

"It's okay, boy. No bath for you. Come on." She patted her lap.

Dash put his head back on her lap and she scratched his ear, smiling.

Later, after the men had bathed, they came into the parlor smelling much better.

Jake had shaven his beard off and trimmed his mustache into a handle bar style.

Carolyn gawked as he walked into the room.

The man was downright handsome beneath all that hair.

His long handlebar mustache made her think of kisses. She wondered if it would tickle.

Matthew, on the other hand, had done none of this. Had not even trimmed his hair or beard. Carolyn was shocked. *Did he have no more respect for mother than that?* All he'd done was wash his beard and hair, which had dampened his shirt. *She's going to be disappointed in him.*

Matt poured both men a glass of whiskey, and then poured Carolyn a glass of sherry, without asking her if she wanted one.

"Here," he said. "You're going to need this before we're done talking."

She reached for the glass, her thoughts on the conversation they needed to have.

He's probably right. I need to tell him all about what happened to Pa and how Mr. Henning Holland is trying to take our ranch. I may need something stronger than sherry for this.

Jake's eyes settled on Carolyn the moment he stepped out of the kitchen and into the hallway outside of the parlor. She looked beautiful sitting in the soft glow of the lamps, her hair lit from behind, making it even more golden, and her clear green eyes looking up at him.

Then she gave him a quick look up and then down, something flaring between them. A spark of attraction, a pull.

She'd gone from being alarmed at the sight of him when they'd first met, to being attracted to him. This was quite an improvement. A slow grin began at the sides of his mouth.

She blushed and glanced away. He liked the fact that he'd made her blush. She was even prettier when she blushed.

Jake watched brother and sister and knew what they'd discuss next would go down better with a drink to follow, if the subject could be gotten down.

Matt gestured to Carolyn to sit and then handed her a glass. "I read what you said in the letter, but I want you to start at the beginning and don't leave anything out. What happened?"

She held the glass, but then put it down and rubbed her hands along her thighs, smoothing her skirt before speaking. Then she inhaled, taking a deep breath, and began. "Mr. Henning Holland claims pa lost the ranch to him in a card game, but you know how pa felt about gambling. I've never seen him play cards. Why, he probably didn't even know how." Carolyn's brow furrowed. "No one in our family plays cards."

"No." Matt shook his head. "He knew how." His gaze grew distant. "I know how."

"You play cards?" Shock filled her face. "When did you start to play cards? How did you learn? Did pa teach you?"

"Wasn't him." Matt shook his head. "Mama's first husband taught me."

Carolyn's eyes widened and she gasped. She held her breath, waiting to hear more.

"Breathe," Jake commanded. Then he said, "Before you faint on us."

She exhaled and then inhaled again. "When, Matt? I've never seen you play."

"I've known how to play since I was seven. Picked it up fast, running with outlaws."

"The bad men taught you. Before the bad things happened." Carolyn nodded, reverting to the language of her childhood.

"No. Mother's first husband did. Before the bad things."

To Jake, it sounded as if they were speaking in childhood codes. And maybe they were. He wondered what 'the bad things' were and just how bad they were.

"Robert Truman knew how to play," Matt said. "But he stopped playing after the bad things. Said he didn't want to upset ma. Didn't want her to think he was like her first husband."

"How bad was he, Matt? Our father."

"Bad enough." Sally's spoke from the doorway where she now stood, having finally left her room. She stood wearing her blue and white floral dressing gown, one hand holding onto the parlor wall, the other pressed flat, formed against her throat as if she couldn't bear to speak of what she would say next. A habit formed before they were born. "Bad enough to hide behind our son when the bullets started flying."

Carolyn gasped. "No. Our own father did that?"

"Yes." Matt gazed into his sister's horror stricken eyes. "He did. Be glad you can't remember."

She gazed back. "You've changed, Matt."

"Yes, I have." He nodded. "And you always were an innocent. Pa did his best to keep you that way."

Jake watched her and knew what Matt said was true. She'd been protected on this ranch ever since she was a child and had a sweet innocence about her. One he would like to see preserved as well.

"I wish things had been different for us," Sally said. "Especially for you, Matthew."

"You did the best you could, mama. None of it was your fault," Matt said. "And you saved my life. You were brave and strong. I remember everything." He rolled his shoulders back as if to shrug something off. "I'm fine. All that is in the past. Now, what else can you tell me about what happened to Pa?"

"He was out moving the cattle from the summer pasture. Getting things ready for winter. He never came home," Sally's voice broke.

"Was there anything that happened in the weeks before? Did he have any trouble here, or anywhere else? Anything he talked about, or was concerned about? Was there anyone he'd had words with who might've still been angry with him?"

"Not that I know of," Sally said. "He hadn't been sleeping well, but I thought it was just his bad knee and his back bothering him, like it does sometimes when the weather is changing."

Matt nodded and then turned to his sister. "Carolyn, do you know of anything?"

"I don't," she said. "Pa had been staying home more than usual."

"Did he say anything about a card game to either of you?"

"No," Sally said. "I've never known him to play cards. It was a shock to hear he'd wagered the ranch."

Matt nodded.

"I don't believe he did," Carolyn said. "He was home at night. That's another reason I don't believe he went to play cards. I mean, when would he have done that? At night he made sure to be home."

"He did go to town once," Sally said. "The week before he was shot, he went to town to get the wagon fixed and since he was going to be home late, we agreed he would eat dinner in town. He said he had dinner and then picked up the wagon and headed on back. That must be the night he went to the card game."

"Even if he went to a card game that night, I don't believe pa would have gambled the ranch," Matt said.

"I don't believe it either," Carolyn said. "Just because Mr. Henning Holland says it happened, doesn't mean it did." She turned to Matt. "You'll look into it won't you? I think Mr. Holland is lying."

CHAPTER 3

"Yes, we'll look into it," Matt said. "I think he's lying too."

"But he has the paper," Sally said. "I saw it. And why would he lie?"

"Think about it mama. Why would pa stop at Mr. Holland's on the way home? For a card game? That's not like pa at all." Carolyn shook her head. "And to lose the ranch and then not tell anyone about it for a week? He never would've done that to you. He wouldn't have done any of that."

"Well he did," Sally said. "Men aren't always honest with their wives. Mr. Henning Holland has the paper and it has Robert's signature on it."

"You're sure it's his?" Matt asked.

"Yes. It looks just like his signature," Sally said sadly. "This is the only time he has let me down in all our years together." He promised me we'd never be homeless again.

"Looks *just like* his signature?" Jake asked. He and Matt exchanged glances, their thoughts likely similar about this.

Signatures could be forged.

"Sounds out of character for him," Jake said.

"Very," Carolyn and Sally spoke at the same time. It was one thing they both agreed on.

"That's one reason not to believe Mr. Holland," Matt said. "I don't believe him."

"He's taking advantage of pa's death to try to steal this ranch," Carolyn said.

"That is very possible," Jake said.

"I don't trust him one bit," Carolyn said.

"You never did like him," Sally said. "Ever since you were little you've taken a dislike to the man, though he has done you no harm. You may not like him, but that doesn't matter. The document is legal; the circuit judge looked at it and said it was. Mr. Henning Holland will force us off this land unless -"

Carolyn held up her hand and spoke, cutting her mother off. "I'm not marrying that man. I won't be forced into it."

"No one is forcing you to do anything," Matt said. "You can stop worrying about that."

Sally wrung her hands, frowning. It was clear she thought a marriage would solve everything. But she was the only one in the room holding that opinion. Jake was not in favor of forced or arranged marriages and if Carolyn didn't want one, he and Matt would make sure she didn't have one.

"Let's say this paper is legal and valid, even though we're sure it's not." Jake said. "If Henning Holland already has rights to the ranch, he's got nothing to coerce you with, so why does he think coercing you to marry him will still work?"

"He says he'll give me the land the morning after our wedding, as a gift," Carolyn said.

Matt snorted. "He hasn't thought this through. The land

would be completely yours as his wife, if he were to leave it to you in his will. Be hard for a dead man to give you anything, unless you're in his will. It would be even harder for a dead man to marry you."

"Matthew!" Sally gasped and her hand rose to her throat again.

He turned to her. "What do you think I do, mama? Chase cows?"

"You're, you're like a sheriff," she said.

He shook his head. "No. We chase outlaws, criminals, Injuns and Mexicans, who are deadly. We have to be even more deadly. Which means being ready to kill. We fight and we kill men. We are judge, jury, jailor and executioner. Sometimes we have to hunt them down and we always bring justice. It's what Texas Rangers do."

"There's been enough killing," Sally said.

"One more won't make any difference," he said with a shrug. "If he's tricked pa, he's a dead man."

"I don't want to hear any more about that," Sally said.

"Not a fit topic for ladies, I agree," Matthew said. "Out of resect for you both, I won't discuss it in your presence again."

"Thank you," Sally said. "Mr. Holland assures me that if Carolyn marries him, everything will be fine. He's also offered to look for Robert's killer, even if it was dangerous cattle rustlers."

Matt snorted at that. "Is he looking now?"

"No, not yet."

"So that's also conditional on a marriage happening. If he really wanted to find who did it, he'd already be looking. Every day that trail grows colder." Matt turned back to Carolyn. "There is only one question here, as far as a wedding, and you are the only one who can answer it. Do you want to marry Mr. Henning Holland?"

"No," she spoke vehemently. "I do not. I will marry for love or not at all."

Jake was glad to hear it. More glad than he cared to let on right now.

"Then that's settled." Matt said. "No more talk about marrying. Both of you can put that topic out of your minds now." His voice was firm and brooked no argument.

Carolyn exhaled a big sigh of relief.

Jake watched her facial features shift and lift as if a huge weight had been lifted. He wished he could lift that weight permanently and would have to see what he could do about that.

"Jake and I are gonna scout around, and see what we can find out about pa's death, and I don't want anyone to know I'm back in town." Matt ran his hand down his beard. "I'm keeping the beard long, so no one will recognize me. This is why I didn't clean up more, mama. Not out of any disrespect for you."

"I did wonder," she said.

"Oh," Carolyn said. "That makes sense now. I wondered too."

"And I'd soon have heard an earful from you about it, I'm sure," he said.

"Why yes, you would have," Carolyn admitted with a nod.

"You two will stay on the ranch. Don't leave it for any reason. If you need something from town, one of us will bring it back for you. I want you here where I know you are safe. Pa's killer could still be nearby."

"Matt, it would be better if you leave the talking to me,"

Jake said. "Outside of this ranch. Someone might recognize your voice."

"Agreed," Matt said.

Jake looked to Carolyn. "You can't let anyone know your brother is home. Or that I'm here. Not yet."

"All right," she said.

"We'll stay here tonight, but then we've got to go," Matt said. "The more days pass, the harder it will be to find pa's killer."

"And when Mr. Henning Holland comes to call?" Sally asked.

"I'll tell him to go home and won't let him in," Carolyn said.

"That would be rude," Sally said. "He'll think I didn't raise you to have good manners."

"I don't care," Carolyn said. "I don't have to be friendly to a man who is trying to take our land. The time for manners is over. I'd like to tell him to go to hell."

"Lord help me, my children have lost all the manners I raised them with and turned into ruffians," Sally said with a shake of her head. "I'm tired and going to bed." She turned to head back to bed.

They watched her go in silence.

Once she'd gone, Matt spoke again. "We'll be gone in the morning, before first light. Before you're even awake. No need for you to fix us breakfast. We're used to taking care of ourselves and I can cook an egg as well as you. We don't want anyone to know we've come through here, so you may need to remind mama that you both have to act like you haven't heard back from me. If they know I've joined the rangers, they won't expect me. People expect rangers to be out on the Texas border and out of touch for long periods of time. So they'll assume I haven't heard about pa yet."

"But Matt, most people don't know you're a ranger," she said. "I don't think anyone knows except me and mamma. Pa and mama were real closed mouthed about where you went."

Matt appeared dumbfounded. "They didn't tell anyone?"

She shook her head. "I don't think so. He was too mad to talk about it and she would just start crying so they both avoided the subject."

"I thought they'd be proud."

"Pa was. He may not have said it, but he was. Mama was just worried about you."

Matt shook his head.

"People at pa's funeral were whispering that you were dead," Carolyn said. "That made me so mad. I can't stand those women gossiping about us and at pa's funeral too."

The expression on Matt's face showed his shock at hearing her words.

Jake said, "This will work in our favor. They won't expect two rangers looking into your pa's death and if they think you're dead, all the better, for now."

"True." Matt nodded, quieter now.

"Well, I'm sure glad you're home." Carolyn threw her arms around her brother. "And I'm glad you're a fearsome ranger, beard and all."

He hugged her back tight. "I missed you too, Carolyn."

Jake stepped out of the parlor, giving them privacy, and went outside to walk the perimeter of the house, his eyes and ears sharp.

If everyone thought the two women lived alone now, and that word spread, it made them more vulnerable to attack. Word like that would always spread and eventually someone would come with a bad motive, wanting one thing or another from the women. Right now, the main thing was to keep them safe while they worked the rest out.

As he walked and took him his surroundings he had time to think.

Carolyn was a beautiful and spirited woman. One he would like to court. He thought of this as he walked past a flower garden, and then he paused at the edge. Taking out his knife, he cut three yellow roses. It was a start. He'd put them in a jar and leave them for Carolyn to find in the morning with a note. He knew just what he wanted to say.

Walking on to complete the circle of the perimeter, he returned to his thoughts.

He understood Matt a whole lot better now. He knew what drove Matt to bring justice to the worst of the 'bad men' and the reason way he reacted the way he did when seeing women and children mistreated. A new respect for Matt rose within him, along with a deeper understanding of his closest friend.

It was a hell of a thing for a man to use his own son as a shield in a gun battle. But that boy had grown to be one hell of a man.

CAROLYN STEPPED INTO THE KITCHEN, feeling how quiet the house was in the early morning light and missing her brother and Jake already. The men had been up and gone before the sun was up. Carolyn had never been one to get up while it was still dark out. She woke along with the sunrise, which felt more natural to her, and like her mother, she had been sleeping more than usual. For a moment though, she wished her brother had awakened her before the men rode out. She'd gladly have risen.

Then she saw the pretty yellow bouquet, which sat waiting for her by the coffee pot with a note. Three yellow roses with a note that said,

Carolyn,

I'm not sure which is prettier, these flowers or your smile. Hope these make you smile until I return. I'd like to see your smile more often.

Jake.

The flowers and the note kept her smiling all day. She even tucked one of the roses into her hair before dinner, hoping the men would make it back tonight, in time for Jake to see her wearing it. He really was the handsomest man she'd ever seen, once he'd shaved that beard off and trimmed his hair and his mustache. She hoped he liked beef stew. She'd made a big pot for dinner in case the men came back. If they didn't, then she and her mother would be eating leftovers for a few days.

She heard thunder off in the distance, the sounds moving closer, which was a sign along with the clouds that had threatened all day to drop rain.

Carolyn dished beef stew into a bowl for Dash and set it aside to cool.

Peering out the window at the darkening sky she saw darkening clouds turning everything gray.

A big storm was coming.

Reaching for a lamp, she found a match, lit it and set the lamp on the table. "Looks like it's going to rain, Dash."

Dash wagged his tail and barked as if in agreement.

"I'm going to go check on mama. Let her know supper is ready."

She turned to go down the hall and Dash followed her. She stopped in front of her mother's door and knocked once. "Mama?" she called softly.

When her mother didn't answer she pushed open the door. The room was dark, but she could see her mother curled up on the bed, sleeping. "Mama, are you hungry? Dinner is ready."

"You go on, dear. Don't wait for me," her mother mumbled. "I'll eat later."

Not entirely sure if her mother was awake, or talking in her sleep, Carolyn eased the door closed again. She glanced down at Dash. "Looks like it's just you and me, boy."

Dash wagged his tail and then followed her back to the kitchen.

She reached for her pa's old rain slicker that still hung by the back door. Putting it on, she paused before going out. Dash was at the door, ready and he woofed.

"I'm not sure I want to have my clean kitchen smelling like wet dog," she said. "I think you should stay here this time." She took the bowl of food and set it down on the floor in the usual place.

Dash looked from the door to the bowl of food and then at her.

"You go ahead and eat, boy. There's no sense you going out and getting all wet."

"Woof," Dash answered her and walked over to his bowl. He looked at her again.

"I won't be gone long. Eat your supper."

Dash wagged his tail and tipped his nose to the stew, and sniffed it before starting to eat.

The stew smelled mighty good to Carolyn as well. The sooner she fed the horses, the sooner she could come back inside and have her supper. Maybe by then mama would be up and would eat with her.

She went outside, looking up at the darkening sky and hurrying toward the barn. The stew she'd made would be welcome tonight if the weather was turning colder, as it tended to do this time of year. The heat of summer could only extend so far into the fall and winter. They were overdue for rain. It had been a long warm, dry season thus far and they needed it. From the looks of the sky they were about to get plenty of rain and already the air was chillier. She planned to dish out two bowls of hot stew for her and mama for their supper after she came back in. Then she'd go wake her mama if she wasn't up yet and make sure she ate. She glanced overhead again and her thoughts turned to the men.

Matt and Jake will be out in this weather, doing God only knew what, but not likely staying inside keeping dry and warm.

She frowned as she opened the door to the barn and slipped inside. Worrying about them had been a constant since they'd left.

Whoever had killed pa might kill them too.

She couldn't help worrying.

Hanging up the slicker, she headed for the first stall. Rain started to patter on the roof and the horses nickered. She figured the approaching storm had them nervous. Thunder crashed in the distance, but nearer this time. The big boom made the horses nervous. She didn't blame them. It had made her jump too.

It didn't take her long to feed three horses as tonight she moved faster than usual, trying to avoid getting caught in a downpour on her way back to the house. The storm had moved in quicker than she'd thought, and now it was dark outside, the rain making everything gray as it poured down. Making the interior of the barn even darker as no light shone through any openings. If she hadn't finished feeding the animals she would have needed to light one of the lanterns. But as she was done, and heading to the house, she didn't bother.

Boom!

Lightning came again, just as Carolyn was just reaching for the rain slicker, so she could head back to the house. She jumped.

As she jumped, the barn door opened behind her and a man stepped inside, his hand closing around her mouth. It all happened so fast in the dark, beneath that boom, that she barely registered it as the shock and surprise of the attack filled her body and mind with panic.

No!

Her eyes widened.

His hand was on her mouth.

She struggled to be free. Both of her hands reached up to try to pry the man's arm down and pull his hand away from her mouth.

His arm was thick and too strong for her to budge.

Another arm wrapped around her midsection, picking her up and yanking her backwards against his chest.

The horses nickered softly, agitated by the fast movements of the man and the thunder and lightning booming and flashing outside.

Dash, left in the house, didn't bark at the men or try to bite them.

Her rifle leaned against the front porch, too far away.

These two facts flashed through her mind at once, in a matter of seconds.

No dog, no gun, no way to call for help, and no one to hear her call.

She'd made every mistake she could have made.

The sound of the door opening behind her, panicked her even more, the knowledge he would try to take her away, out that door, with the help of a second man who'd opened that door making her wriggle hard, fighting with every muscle in her body.

But the man who had grabbed her never let go, or lessened his grip. Instead, he held tighter as he dragged her away from the barn door.

Lightning flashed again, while the door was open, giving her a glimpse of two men.

One wore a red bandanna around his neck. He had dark, tan skin, black greasy hair, and looked to be Mexican. The other one, a red headed younger man had to be one of the skinniest she'd ever seen.

They came inside and closed the door, shutting in the four of them together.

"Get her feet," the man holding her ordered briskly. His voice was strong, but soft. There was hard iron in there, but it was smooth iron, too.

The Mexican wearing the red bandana knelt quickly, a length of rope in his hand.

Carolyn tried to kick, but she was still being held up on her tiptoes.

The man with the rope deftly caught her feet, looping the rope several times around her booted ankles, cinching them tight with a quick knot.

The skinny redhead was looking through a crack in the boards towards the house.

With a fluid twist, the man holding Carolyn turned, laying her on the ground face down, knocking the wind out of her, the flower falling out of her hair onto the ground. As he laid her down, his grip on her mouth loosened and she tried to scream again, but it was no good.

The roping man was on top of her, holding her legs and

hips still, while he pulled her arms behind her back and crossed her wrists, ready to tie them.

"No. Tie them in front," the first man said. "She'll have to ride."

The Mexican roping her turned her over.

Rough rope slid across her skin as he bound her hands in front of her.

She struggled, her panic making her start to hyperventilate.

Her wrists now secured, the man holding her head and mouth, reached up with one hand and took a white handkerchief from his pocket. He then slipped it under his hand deftly into her mouth, holding it in place while he took a blue and white bandanna and put it between her parted teeth.

The cloth, dry against her mouth, pressed against her tongue, making it impossible for her to speak.

He tightened a cruel knot behind her head, which pressed, letting her know this cloth would not come loose. "Got her," he said.

The Mexican who'd roped her rose away from them.

The first man stood, picking up Carolyn easily. As she settled, she got her first good look at the man who had grabbed her. He wore a black shirt, black pants and boots which made him hard to see in the dark. He had dark hair and intelligent blue eyes.

For a moment she stood on bound ankles, but then the man bent forward, putting his shoulder in her midsection and wrapping an arm around her legs. When he straightened, Carolyn was bent over his shoulders.

She gave a last, desperate wriggle, but the Mexican who had roped and tied her stepped in front of her and caught the underside of her chin.

Carolyn froze as he brought a big Bowie knife from his belt up in front of her eyes.

"Enough of that," he growled, his voice gravelly, with a hint of Spanish accent. "We're not supposed to hurt you, but that don't mean we can't have a little fun either. This ride can be heaven or hell, *Chiquita*. Understand?"

Her terrified eyes wide, Carolyn just barely managed a small, tight nod against his hand.

The knife abruptly vanished, and he released her jaw.

The redhead who'd been watching the house turned away nervously. "Let's go."

Silently, the three men went further into the barn, to the big double doors that opened out the other side. They opened them enough to pass through, then closed the doors behind them and made their way to four horses tied to the branches of nearby trees.

How did I not see or hear four horses and three riders approaching? I've allowed worry to distract me. And now there really is something to worry about.

Two of the men mounted. The third draped Carolyn over the saddle of the fourth horse. Her hair hung down, as her head was upside down on one side of the horse and on the other side, her legs dangled. When the third man mounted, they all turned their horses and began making their silent ride into the night.

Rain sprinkled down upon them as thunder boomed, closer than before. A flash of lightning lit the sky briefly, bright and then was gone. She didn't know how they could see where they were going and wondered if they were already familiar with the route. She didn't like being out in the storm with lightning flashing, which was almost as frightening as being kidnapped. She hoped it did not hit her while crossing the open pastures.

The horses moved across the pasture, carrying the three determined riders and one frightened one, until they were off of the Nightingale Ranch and entering the wooded area to the back of the property.

Carolyn, soaked from the rain and chilled from the temperature dropping, wished she had the rain slicker hanging in the barn. It was a cold, chilling rain and her hair and her dress were soaked. Both clung to her body. The night air had cooled and she could not get warm. She began to shiver and her teeth clattered together. She closed her eyes and prayed that her brother and his friend would find her soon. She wanted nothing more than to be back home in her warm bed again where she was safe, and loved. Her mother would be worried sick.

Sprinkles turned heavier, until it was a downpour, water running down Carolyn's neck and into her eyes and nose. She twisted her head trying to keep the rain out and coughed.

"She's choking," the first man, who seemed to be the leader, said. "We need to stop."

She needed to not be with her head upside down on a horse and she needed that slicker hanging in the barn. Needed to be out of this rain and away from these men. How or where she didn't know, but she had to get away from them. She'd wait for any chance she could take and be ready for it.

Each step the horse took brought her further and further from the safety of her home and made the chance of Matt and Jake finding her, slimmer by the minute.

They stopped near a cluster of trees and the Mexican lifted her up and then set her on the ground, on her feet.

She was dizzy at first and didn't realize what he was doing until he reached down with his knife, flipped it open

47

and slit her skirts. Then he cut the ties binding her ankles and lifted her back on the horse. This time he tied her hands to the saddle horn.

Louder booms came nearly overhead, followed by a fast downpour that hit hard onto their heads and shoulders.

"Damn it," the leader cursed into the rain. "We need to get out of this rain."

"I know a line shack near here." The Mexican with the Spanish accent spoke, his voice loud as he shouted over the rain.

She cringed as rain ran down her neck and over her clothes, soaking her even more. The cold chill of the air and water made her shiver.

"Good," the leader said. "Where?"

"About half a mile southeast," the Mexican shouted again.

"We'll head there."

The Mexican turned his horse, taking the lead as the others followed.

Through the dark downpour she could see the line shack up ahead. The small log shack had no door, but a cowhide covered the opening. It had a sod roof and its logs shone black-brown in the rain. The lean to beside it would offer shelter for the horses.

They reached the shack and dismounted. The Mexican took her down off the horse and pushed her inside the line shack, while the other men put the horses in the lean to.

Inside the shack it was dark and cold.

Rain dripped from the sod roof into the room in spots here and there, making the room damp and musty smelling.

A cold drop fell onto Carolyn's forehead and she tried to dodge the next drop by leaning to the side.

The Mexican, mistaking her movement for an attempt to

pull away, yanked her arm, moving her back beneath the drips.

"You ain't going nowhere," he said. "Best you get used to that."

The other two men stepped inside, out of the rain.

Another drip hit her forehead again and she shivered.

The leader, noting the raindrops now running down the side of her face, grabbed a chair and swung it around near her. "Sit," he said.

Carolyn's eyes narrowed. "I'm not a dog," she said, glaring at him. "Don't tell me to sit."

He laughed.

Her eyes narrowed even more but this time kept her thoughts to herself.

He's enjoying this. I can't give him the satisfaction.

The redhead had moved to watch out the door, and was standing in the doorway, peering out from the hide covering the doorway, trying to see through the rain.

Thunder and lightning crashed overhead, bringing a bright flash of light.

"Feed the horses," the Mexican said. "Grain's in the corner."

Carolyn had noticed there was a well inside the shack. The shack had been built right over it. That was mighty convenient, but it also meant no one had to leave to find water.

She was surprised to note that what had looked like an abandoned shack from the outside was actually well stocked for provisions. Not only was there water and grain for the horses, there was a tin of coffee and other tins of food provisions.

Did the owner of this shack know these men were hiding out here in his shack?

"Slade, how long do you think this rain will keep up?" the redhead asked.

The leader gave him a sharp look.

Yes, now I know your name, Carolyn thought. If I can get free, I know who to tell the sheriff about.

"No telling." The leader said. "Keep watching. See if anyone has followed." His tone showed his unhappiness with the younger man.

"You ain't no good to us standing in that doorway," the Mexican said. "Feed them horses and then get your ass out there in them woods, where you belong. Like I told you. Out of sight."

The redhead filled a scoop with grain and carried it out to the horses.

Slade approached Carolyn, stood in front of her for a moment, looking down at her.

She looked up at him, wondering what he would do next.

He knelt and reached for her ankles. His hands reached around her ankles and began moving up.

She gasped.

CHAPTER 4

"*T*ake your hands off me," Carolyn said.

"Quiet. I'm checking," the leader said.

"Checking for what?"

"Gun," he said.

"I don't carry a gun."

"That remains to be seen," he said. "Those little tavern pistols you women like to carry can be hidden in small places."

"I do not have a pistol," she said.

His hands kept moving up her legs, up and up, fingers busy checking everything.

She gasped at the familiarity.

The Mexican laughed. She didn't like the look the Mexican gave her or his dirty laugh.

"Stop touching me. Stop touching my clothes," she said. "Take your filthy hands off me."

"It has to be done," the leader said. "Can't have you shoot me or the other men the minute I turn my back."

"I told you I don't have a gun."

"So you did." He nodded. "But women lie."

His hands moved up her body, as he continued checking for weapons.

She leaned back away from him, leaning against the chair. But nothing she did slowed his assault of her body. She gasped and gasped again as he touched her.

"Be quiet," he said. "I'm not hurting you."

The Mexican spoke. "I want some of that."

The leader gave him a sharp look. "No. You know our orders."

"Si, si. He pays well for a virgin. So we give him his virgin."

The blood drained from her face, as she understood.

Whoever hired them to take me wants a virgin. I'm only safe until they give me to him.

"She's fully clothed, or I wouldn't be touching her. And I'm only patting her down."

"And taking your time about it," she said.

He flashed her a smile some women would consider handsome. "I enjoy my work."

Hurry Matt. Oh please God, let him hurry.

She didn't trust that the Mexican would stay away from her if the leader weren't around. The way he was looking at her, she would not trust that at all.

Carolyn began to shiver.

"Can't have her taking sick," the leader said. "Get her a blanket."

The Mexican pulled out a saddle blanket from the pile in the corner where they'd dumped their things in a hurry to get inside. He moved over to her and placed it around her shoulders.

The damp blanket smelled of horse and was none too clean, but it provided some warmth and kept some of the drippy rain off of her. Rain continued to pour down outside.

She hoped it would never let up and Matt would find her before the men took her further away. No thunderstorm would stop her brother. He was fearless and he would never give up.

The leader opened the stove and piled a few dry logs inside, along with kindling. He took a tin box that sat on the stove and opening it, found matches. Lighting one, he then lit the fire and prodded at it with a steel poker until heat began to come off of it. "Be here long enough to make coffee," he said. "It will warm you up."

"I don't drink coffee," she said.

He gave her a look of disbelief.

"I drink tea."

"No tea here, sister," he said.

"I am not your sister," she said. "And you are not my brother. I have a brother and he is a far better man than you."

"Nevertheless, tonight you will drink coffee." He brought the subject back to the coffee and ignored what she'd said about her brother.

She pursed her lips, determined to do nothing she didn't have to do. Coffee was something she had no taste for.

Inside the line shack was a well and the Mexican hauled up a bucket of water. Carolyn had never been inside of a building that had a well in it. But she supposed that at least the water would be clean. She still wasn't interested in drinking coffee, but maybe they would let her have some fresh water. She watched as Slade poured water into the coffee pot and then set it on the heat to boil. He seemed a more civilized, more educated man than the other two; from the way he moved to the way he spoke.

When the coffee was ready, she refused the cup Slade poured for her.

He set her cup on the table and taking his own coffee cup, walked to the doorway and stood looking out. He kept his back to her, ignoring her, and seemed to be watching the rain.

Tired as she was, she didn't sleep all night.

Slade stood at the doorway looking out, watching for the weather to change. He stood watching all night and paced when he wasn't standing still.

About an hour before the sun came up, the rain slowed to a sprinkle. He said, Let's go."

His men to prepared to ride out again.

She wondered where they were taking her and why they'd kidnapped her. She hoped Matt and Jake would find her soon.

MATT AND JAKE, determined to learn all they could about Robert Truman's death, and why Mr. Henning Holland wanted the Truman ranch so badly, rode toward town before the sun was up. Since the people of Nacogdoches likely didn't know Matt, they didn't split up, but they would be wary because there was always the chance that someone who knew Matt would come to town for supplies or to do business.

Jake headed to the saloon to start making inquiries and Matt took the horses to the stables. Rain had been steady all day with thunderstorms moving in and both men were ready for a drink. Once he saw the horses were cared for, Matt would join Jake in the saloon, drinking whisky and learning what they could.

He bellied up to the bar and ordered a shot of whiskey. An older brunette in a red dress watched him for a moment.

He made eye contact with her and nodded. She smiled back at him then gestured to the other women in the room. "See anything you like?" she asked.

"Why yes, ma'am. I do," he said, keeping his gaze on her.

A brief show of surprise crossed her face, but she quickly masked it and gave him a deep smile. The bar tender set a shot of whiskey in front of him. "Hold up," Jake said to him and he then looked at the lady. "Add whatever she's having."

"Thank you," she said and nodded to the bartender who knew what her drink of choice was. The bar tender poured her a glass of brandy.

They both drank.

"You're new in town," she said.

"Yes," Jake said. "This is my first visit."

"Business or pleasure?" she asked.

He knew she had seen his badge. He didn't try to hide it. "This trip is purely personal," he said. "I hear there's ranch land to be had, for the right price."

"Don't know where you heard that," she said. "But they gave you incorrect information. Outdated information. What land was for sale has been bought up."

"All of it?" He frowned. "I heard otherwise."

"Mister, you want to know about land, you can ask at the land office, but he's going to tell you the same as I am. A lot of people sold out to Henning Holland. He owns the biggest spread around these parts and it's grown bigger."

"Interesting. What does Holland do with all this land?"

"He runs cattle on it. Big operation."

"Well now. That is disappointing news. Thank you for letting me know."

"My pleasure," she said. "Happy to be of help."

"Another," he called to the bartender. "And for the lady?" He looked at her, questioning.

She smiled and nodded a yes.

He spoke again as the bartender refilled their drinks.

"It may be a waste of time, but I believe I'll go on over to the land office in the morning, just to be sure he hasn't left a parcel out. I'd still like to buy a piece of land if there's one to be had."

"Best to leave that alone right now," she said.

"Why?"

She leaned in close to his ear as if to whisper sweet nothings and spoke low, "Railroad is coming through. Men with more money than Henning Holland are making big deals."

"Why are you telling me this?" he answered low, so she had to stay close to her.

She leaned back, looked him over, head to toe; in a way that warmed him as it would have warmed any red blooded man. "I'd hate to see a man like you poke his nose into the wrong tree when it holds a hornet's nest. Come upstairs and forget about all that tonight."

Matt had to choose that moment to walk into the bar. He glanced about the room, saw Jake and headed straight for him.

"You have a friend looking for you," she said.

Jake turned to look where she was looking. She was as sharp as many rangers he knew, not missing a thing in this establishment.

"Two Texas rangers in town?" She gazed directly into Jakes eyes. "On, personal business?"

He could hear the questioning doubt, the mistrust, which had formed, and that she wasn't buying that he was here alone on a personal matter. "Not here to arrest anyone," he said. "No warrants out on anyone in this town. We're just passing through."

"Good." She nodded. "You'll tell me before there's any shooting." It was more command than request. The woman was not intimidated by them, and expected a mutual respect.

"Yes ma'am." He nodded, giving her that respect, but then paused before speaking again. "Unless some fool decides to draw."

"Now what kind of fool would draw on a Texas Ranger?" she asked.

"You'd be surprised." Matt said. He'd stepped up to the bar on the other side of Jake.

"Would have to be a very drunk fool," she said.

"Yes, ma'am," Matt said.

She nodded, and finished her drink.

Thunder crashed loud outside, lightning striking in the middle of the street. Everyone saw it through the windows as it illuminated everything briefly.

"I believe that's our cue that we'll be needing a room for the evening," Jake said. "I'm not going out to ride, or camp in that."

"Me either," Matt said.

"You have a room for us?" Jake asked.

"That I do," the woman said.

"I didn't catch your name," Jake said. "I'm Jacob Brace, but you can call me Jake."

"Hello Jake, nice to meet you," she said. "I'm Pearl."

"Pleased to meet you," he said. "This is my friend Matt."

Matt nodded his head at her. "Ma'am."

"Well. I'll leave you two men to your whiskey." She looked directly at Jake again. "If you need me later, send one of the girls upstairs for me."

"Will do." Jake nodded and gave her his most charming smile.

I might get more information from her later.

Whores often knew more of what went on in town than anyone gave them credit for. Drunken men would talk and those men often spilled their guts to a whore. Some even paid the women to just listen to them for a while before or after sex.

He waited until she went upstairs to talk to Matt, and spoke low enough no one else could hear.

"I know why Holland wants your ranch," Jake said. "You're sitting on five hundred acres of timber and pasture lands. That's a good solid thing to be sitting on when a railroad is coming through."

"Railroad?" Matt said.

"Yep." Jake called the bartender over. "Another for me and one for my friend." This would be his last drink tonight. He needed to stay sober, especially if he was going to be talking to the woman again, later tonight.

As the bartender poured their drinks, Jake asked, "What can you tell me about the railroad coming through here? That will bring many new things to the surrounding towns." He slid money across the bar toward the man.

The bar tender looked down at the money. Then with no expression on his face, he pocketed the money and it was as gone as if it had never been there. He said, "I've got a railroad story for ya. Railroad survey crew came through here. Crossed Angelina County, planning a route for the line. Well, the surveying crew went carousing on a Saturday night, got a little rowdy in a saloon over in Homer and then the constable put them in jail. After they got out, the chief of the crew was so angry that he ordered them to find a route that would bypass Homer and go by Denman Springs. And since Denman and his son hosted the crewmembers for a few days...."

Jake and Matt both laughed at the man's story, as he'd expected them to.

"That's a fine story," Jake said. "And good whiskey too."

The man gave him a nod and then moved on down to the other end of the bar to wait on other customers.

"So that railroad is coming through Denman's land and Holland is buying land up," Jake said. "I'll bet he's planning to sell to the railroad if he hasn't already."

"That doesn't make sense. They'll just take the land for the railroad if they want it," Matt said. "You know they will."

"Not necessarily," Jake said. "Not if someone has cut a deal. Think about all the wood they'll need to lay that track and wood for the engines. Then the buildings they'll build for all those train stations. You're sitting pretty with the land, the timber and a small herd of cattle."

"Why didn't they offer us this deal? Why offer it to Holland?"

"Back room deals more than likely."

Matt cursed.

"You know how that works. I'd bet Holland is in with the railroad men," Jake said. "But we don't have proof. We need to see the land deeds and find out exactly what Holland has done."

"Damn. Holland is behind this, I'm sure of it. Pa would never have gambled the ranch."

"We'll ask about your Pa while we're here," Jake said. "But not right away. Give it some time. We just got here."

Matt had downed his drink and now asked for another.

Jake was done drinking so he just leaned against the bar and took in the surroundings. He knew others in the saloons watched him as much as he watched them. Word would spread that two Texas Rangers were in town. Hopefully no one would pull anything stupid and they'd have a quiet night, finish conducting their business and then get on back to the ranch tomorrow. From this point on, Jake would be watching, not drinking. He didn't need another drink.

One of them needed to stay clear headed and Jake had not just lost his father to a gunman, nor was his family losing their land. If Matt wanted to knock back a few or even more than a few, Jake would watch his back and give him the room to do so without comment.

Two hours later, Matt was drunker than Jake had ever seen him. Matt had decided to play poker and was at the table having a winning hand when some fool decided to draw on him.

Matt's gun was out before the other man's hand was halfway done. Even drunk, Matt was a formidable gunman. Sober, he was unstoppable and could shoot with both hands equally as well, with one gun or two.

"Stop." Jake stepped up and placed his hand on Matt's arm. "Think of the mess."

To the other man he said, "Holster that."

The man, who clearly wasn't the gunman Matt was, put his gun away and left.

"No harm done," Jake said.

"He called me a cheat," Matt said with a deep frown. "I ain't no cheat."

Pearl stood at the railing of the second floor, surveying the room, and looking down on them. She'd appeared as if she'd sensed trouble and she was watching them now, to see what they would do. Fetching as she was, Jake wouldn't be spending the night with her.

"Of course you're no cheat. He's just a sore loser," Jake said. "Put your gun away. Time we called it an evening,"

Jake said, and as Matt put his gun away and took his winnings, Jake placed an arm around Matt to help him up the stairs to their room. "We'll get a fresh start in the morning."

Matt squinted at him. "I'm fine. There's nothing wrong with me." But with the first step he took, he stumbled.

"If you get sick on me, I'll shoot you myself," Jake said. But he said not another word because he knew from experience.

It did no good to argue with an angry man or a drunk. Likely Matt wouldn't remember much of this tomorrow morning.

He nodded to Pearl as they passed her. "Good night," he said.

"Good night rangers," she replied.

THE NEXT MORNING, Matt was sending up deep snores, the kind that only a man who'd been drinking can send up.

Jake watched him for a moment and then shook his head. He got up, washed at the washbasin and then toweled off before reaching for his boots and the rest of his clothes. Donning them, he grabbed his hat and then stepped out into the hall.

A saloon was a mighty quiet place in the early hours of the morning.

Jake planned to head on over to the land surveyor's office this morning to look over what records they had on the Truman ranch and have that taken care of before Matt was even awake.

Stepping up onto the porch of the building, Jake removed his hat and shook water off of it before placing it back on his head. Pushing the door open, he stepped inside.

"Good morning," the man behind the counter said. "Mighty wet out there."

"Good morning," Jake said. "That it is." He nodded. "Are you the land surveyor?"

"I'm the land clerk. Surveyor isn't in. What can I do for you?"

"I'm interested in the records on the Truman ranch," he said.

The man hesitated. "And you are?"

Jake showed the man his badge.

The man's eyes widened. "What is your interest in the Truman ranch?"

"I heard it might be for sale," he said. "I want to look the records over before speaking to the widow."

"Well now," the man behind the big desk hesitated in his answer and in his manner. "It will take me a while to get that information. Why don't you go on and get some breakfast, or a cup of coffee across the street at Mae Belles Country Cooking, and then come back afterward."

"All right. I'll do that." Jake nodded at him and then stepped outside again.

The man knew something and he was acting nervous.

Jake went into Mae Belles, sat at a table and ordered a cup of coffee. He knew when the little man was watching and behaved as if he didn't.

The thin little man stepped outside, looked right and then left before hurrying down the street as if he was being pursued.

He's in a hurry. Seems like I might've lit a fire under the man. Jake mused to himself as he drained half the coffee; he left payment, and then went outside.

He followed the man down the street and stepped into an alley when the man turned to go up the steps to the telegraph office. The man glanced up and down the street before stepping inside.

So he's sending a telegram to someone. And that someone would soon know a Texas Ranger is making inquiries. That should stir things up.

He waited til the man left the telegraph office, again hurrying back toward his office. Then he stepped out of the alley, and went into telegraph office. "I'd like to send a telegraph," he said.

The telegraph clerk pointed to a pad on a table nearby. "Print out what it's to say and then bring it to me," he said. "We charge you by the letter."

Jake nodded and then went to the table and bent over it, acting as if he would write something. Instead he was really looking at the indentations where the little man had pressed his message hard as he wrote. Taking a pencil, Jake shaded over the indentations.

Mr. Holland,

Texas Ranger inquiring Truman ranch.

JB

That was enough. Holland was in with the land agent. And now he knew a Texas Ranger was looking into things. Jake still wanted to see the records. He looked up at the telegraph clerk who was watching him. "Changed my mind on sending that message," he said. Then he nodded his head, turned and walked out the door.

Heading back to the land office, Jakes wheels were turning as his thoughts turned.

What if Holland had killed Matt's pa? Over the land? Range wars in this part of Texas could get ugly. Holland wouldn't be the first to kill over land.

Back at the land office he stepped inside and said, "What have you got for me?"

The man pushed a survey map on the desk forward where Jake could see the map better. The man pointed to the northern edge of the Truman ranch. "This is where the property starts," he said. Then he ran his finger along it. "It's not a large spread."

"No, not compared to this one," Jake pointed to land he knew belonged to Holland. "Who owns this?"

"Mr. Henning Holland," he said.

"He's got a large spread." Jake's eyes quickly scanned the surrounding lands. "He bought this too?" He pointed to a spread to the east of Holland's ranch, where one name had a line through it and Henning Holland's name written below.

"Yes, sir. He did." The clerk said.

"How are the water rights around this one?" Jake asked. He knew a thing or two about what ranchers would fight over and water was one of the biggest.

"I wouldn't know. You'd have to ask Mr. Holland," the man said with smile.

"Is the Truman ranch still in the widow's name?" Jake asked.

"No." The clerk said. "It's not for sale. The land is already in transfer to Mr. Holland."

"Now how can that be, when the husband just passed?" Jake asked. "The land hasn't had time to be sold, with the husband just put in the ground."

The clerk smiled. "Mr. Holland won that ranch in a poker game."

"You don't say."

"That's right. He won the land and is in the process of settling the paperwork."

"Sounds like you've saved me some time," Jake said. "Thank you kindly."

"Not at all," the man said. "Glad I could clear things up."

But despite his polite words, the man had sweat on his brow and under his arms.

He is a nervous fellow. And clearly lying about something.

Jake headed out the door and over to the saloon where he planned to make sure Matt was up and moving. It was time they headed back to the ranch to tell Sally and Carolyn Truman what they had learned.

THE MEN RODE for Matthew's home, knowing that their next step needed to be looking closer at Holland and his business associates. Men would do crazy things when big money was involved.

The sun was setting when they approached the house, something wasn't right. There were no lights lit and no smoke coming from the chimney. They were hoping for a hot home cooked meal tonight.

Jake and Matt looked at each other and now silent but communicating without words, they dismounted, taking their rifles. Leaving their horses, they approached the house with caution, guns ready, alert for trouble.

As they came closer, Sally called out, "Who's there?"

CHAPTER 5

"*D*on't shoot, Mama, it's me," Matt yelled.

Matt's mother was seated just inside the front door on a parlor chair she'd placed there, with a shotgun in her hands. "Matt?" she called out in the dark. "Is that you?"

"Yes, it's Matt! What's going on? Why are you sitting there in the dark with a shotgun? Where's Carolyn?"

"Carolyn isn't with you?"

"No. I haven't seen her."

"Then she really is gone. They took her," she said, laying the gun across her lap, facing it away from him. She started to sob.

Matt frowned. "Who took her?" Taking the shotgun away from his mother, he checked to see if the shotgun was loaded, and then shook his head and sent Jake a glance as he handed the gun to him.

Jack took the gun and checked it again. Both men liked to verify for themselves the state of any gun they handled. Details like this had kept them alive.

The gun wasn't loaded. Good thing Mrs. Truman hadn't

needed to shoot someone. Maybe she'd been capable with a gun when she was younger, but right now, in her grief, she wasn't doing a good job of looking after herself. She'd forgotten to load the shotgun. At least she hadn't tried to shoot anyone with it. She could've gotten hurt when they realized it was empty.

Mrs. Truman still hadn't answered Matt. She just sat there, sobbing into her hands.

Jake leaned the shotgun against the wall in the corner, near the door, in case it was needed later, after they'd reloaded it.

"Mama, who took Carolyn?" Matt repeated the question in a stronger tone.

Jake understood his frustration. They needed answers and Mrs. Truman crying wasn't helping things.

"I don't know." She wailed the words.

"Okay mama. We'll find her." Matt put his hand on her elbow to help her up. "Come into the kitchen with me, and tell us what happened."

In the dark room Jake lit lamps while Matt settled his mother into a kitchen chair. "Now tell me," Matt said in a firm voice. "From the beginning."

"She went out to the barn to feed the animals, and she left her -," Mrs. Truman choked on her tears.

"Her what?" Matt said.

But she couldn't answer, only cry.

"When mama? When did they take her?" Frustration filled Matt's voice.

Jake knew Matt wanted to kill someone right about now and he was angry, but he was turning his anger toward his mother.

"Take a breath Mrs. Truman, and then tell us," Jake said.

She took a deep breath and then spoke again. "Her rain slicker. Was hanging. Barn." she started to sob harder.

"It was raining and she left her rain slicker in the barn?" Jake asked.

She nodded and cried harder.

"Where's Dash?" Matt asked, his tone still agitated. "He's always with her."

Jake stirred the coal in the fireplace to relight the fire, the action giving him a place for his own anger to go as he listened. He hoped like hell no one had shot that beautiful dog. He hoped no one had harmed Carolyn.

"He was in the kitchen, whining to go out. She didn't call me for breakfast." Mrs. Truman shook her head. "Hadn't cooked any."

"You skipped supper, didn't check on her til morning, until you were hungry." Matt said in a flat voice. "Then you figured out she was missing."

"Well yes, I, I did. I knew she was fixing stew for dinner, but I didn't eat any. I could smell it, but I wasn't hungry. I went to sleep. But then, this morning, she never called me."

"You two were supposed to look out for each other while we were away." Matt's tone was full of criticism and the color in his neck was red and rising along with his temper. "It's your fault we don't know when she was taken."

"I know it," she said, crying harder. "I know it."

"If you'd had that shotgun loaded and been paying attention, this might not have happened."

Watching the situation between mother and son bubbling out of control, Jake interrupted. "They could've taken her at supper time. That's a whole day ahead of us, but we'll find her." He looked out the kitchen window. "Breakfast was a long time ago. Where's the dog now?"

"He wanted to go out. I let him and then I went to the barn to look for her. He didn't follow me." Mrs. Truman started crying again. "I don't know where he is. Run away, I guess."

"Dash would never run away," Matt said.

"Do you think he would've followed her?" Jake asked, knowing some dogs would do that.

"I'm not sure." Matt said. "Border collies don't have the best noses."

"They're not dogs for tracking, true, but their eyes are keen," Jake said. "And he's her dog, isn't he?" He'd noticed as he was speaking that the back door was cracked open a little. He went to close it.

"No!" Mrs. Truman said, sharp and loud. "We have to leave that open, so Dash will come home." Her tone changed. "When Carolyn comes home, she'll expect him to greet her." She nodded, as if it was a fact, Carolyn's coming home. As if her mind had shifted.

Matt and Jake looked at each other. It sounded to Jake as if Matt's mother needed looking after, as her mind might be mixed up. Shock could do strange things to an older person.

"You must bring her back home, Matt," Mrs. Truman said. "I can't lose her too."

"I will, mama."

"Then all she has to do is marry that nice Mr. Henning Holland and everything will be fine again."

"Let's not talk about that any more tonight, momma. When did you last eat?"

"I can't rightly recall," her voice trailed off.

"I'll heat up the stew."

"Not for me. I can't eat that." Mrs. Truman shook her head.

"Why not? Carolyn's cooking hasn't turned bad, I hope."

"It was the last meal she ever made for me." His mother began to cry again. "I just can't."

"All right then," Matt said. "I'm going to cook some eggs and I expect you to eat them."

"Fry 'em with some bacon and I will," she said.

"That's a deal." He nodded.

"I'm going out to take care of the horses," Jake said. "And look around." Matt would've known he would go take care of the horses and if it had been just the two of them, Jake wouldn't have needed to announce it, but it just seemed more polite with Mrs. Truman there and it also let them know they'd have some privacy for a time.

The men had left their horses in front of the house, hurrying inside to see what was wrong, and now the horses needed to be taken care of.

Jake picked up one of the lanterns and carried it outside with him, whistling softly in case the dog was near enough to hear.

No dog came running.

He wouldn't be surprised if the dog had followed tried to find Carolyn, as he was her dog, and border collies were very smart.

Jake looked for tracks as he walked, holding the lantern out to allow him to see the ground. The sooner he started tracking, the sooner they'd find her. He'd check out the barn before he put the horses away for the night, so their tracks wouldn't be added to the mix.

It was a dark night with the moon behind clouds, limiting his vision. The lantern shined light across the ground. Outside the barn, rain hadn't washed away the tracks and the soft ground outside the barn made it easier to see them.

Tracks from what looked like three men, along with their horses, and a fourth horse with no rider was what he found. Jake was certain. Tracking and hunting were things the men in his family did well.

Now he had to attend to the horses. They were tired, hungry and needed to rest before they could be ridden again tomorrow. You could only push a horse so far, and whoever had taken Carolyn had left the barn empty. No horses, no dog and no Carolyn.

It was far too quiet.

Matt wasn't going to like this. He would want to switch horses and take off now. But that wasn't possible.

Hoping the barn would hold clues to Carolyn's disappearance, Jake entered. His thoughts were on Carolyn, remembering how she'd stood up to him and Matt when they first arrived.

She wouldn't have gone along easily. She would've fought being taken.

Jake's jaw set with anger. *Whoever took her had better not have hurt her.*

He had anger all his own, and as he fed the horses, he felt a strong urge to hurt the people who'd taken her, along with the urge to protect Carolyn and a strong desire to save her. He'd never wanted to save anyone so bad in his life.

He saw the rain slicker hanging near the door. Saw where there had been a scuffle, where larger, male footprints surrounded her small footprints. And off to the side, a crushed yellow rose on the barn floor.

He froze. The sight stunned him.

Had she been wearing the flower? Carrying it?

The fact she'd had the flower with her meant she'd liked the flowers he'd given her, and maybe they had made her smile. But she likely wouldn't be wearing that beautiful smile now. He placed the smashed, stemless flower in his shirt pocket.

Normally cool under extreme circumstances, Carolyn's abduction now felt personal for him.

The flower had meant something to her, and that meant something to him. Something he wouldn't have said and perhaps couldn't have put into words.

Now, where was she? And where was her dog? Had Dash gone after his owner?

Once the horses were settled for the night, Jake stepped back outside to search the ground one more time before heading back into the house.

Rain had made the ground soft, so Jake was able to see the tracks of four horses and riders. He began to follow the tracks through the rain, but only got so far when he lost the trail.

"Damn," he spoke into the dark. "I wish the moon would come out from behind those clouds."

But it wasn't to be. Though he rode for a while more, he didn't find them again.

Back in the house, Matt was waiting up for him and pacing.

"What did you find?" His words were out the minute Jake opened the door.

"I found signs of a scuffle and followed their tracks. Didn't get far without a horse."

"Why didn't you saddle one of ours?" Matt frowned deeper.

"None in the barn. None except ours."

"Damn." Matt cursed. He had to know this meant no fresh mounts for them to ride and the possible theft of the horses.

"We'll have to pick up the trail in the morning when visibility is better," Jake said.

"No. I want to go now. Every minute we lose, they can take her further away."

"I understand the urgency. I feel it too. But we need to be smart about this." Jake shook his head. "Remember when we were tracking Black Eyed Sanchez?"

Matt gave a sharp nod.

"We lost his trail and kept on in the direction he seemed to be heading. Took us two weeks to find him. We can't make that mistake with Carolyn. If we lose their trail now, we might not pick it back up."

"You're right," Matt grumbled. "But damn it!" He banged his fist on the table. "I just want to find those sons a bitches and get her home safe before something worse happens."

"I hear you. But we can't mess this up, Matt, we got to do this right." Jake picked up the coffee pot and looked into it and then looked at the empty skillet. "I want to find her as bad as you do. We'll set out before first light and start where the trail left off as soon as the sun is up."

Matt reluctantly nodded his agreement.

"I see you didn't leave me any eggs. And the coffee is almost cold."

"Didn't figure you'd want cold eggs either, when you can have fresh." Matt reached for the skillet. "Go wash up. I'll cook you some. Unless you want stew."

"Thank you," Jake said. "I'll try some of that good stew. No need to cook for me. And after I eat, I'll wash the dishes." Matt had enough to do, looking after his mother, without adding in cooking and doing dishes for Jake as well.

"Appreciate that," Matt said.

"Your mamma doing okay?" Jake asked.

"She is now. Threw a fit about closing that back door. She's sure Dash is coming back and will walk through that door again. I suspect she hopes Carolyn will walk through the door with him. Then I made the mistake of moving pa's chair. That really set her off." He shook his head. "I did get her to eat. She likes my cooking and has settled down now and gone to sleep."

"Good. I hope she's better in the morning before we ride out."

MATT NODDED. "ME TOO."

Jake moved toward the washstand to wash his hands, thoughts of Carolyn on his mind.

"HURRY UP," Slade said, as Carolyn went to relieve herself behind a tree and two bushes. Though they'd ridden out an hour before sunrise, he seemed to be pushing them to move at a fast pace. "We've wasted enough time."

She hurried and soon they were back in their saddles.

After many hours, they stopped again and she was able to walk for a few minutes. Then the Mexican grabbed her and Slade put the gag in her mouth again.

We must be getting near people, she thought. *He must not want me to be able to call out.* She was wet, aching from being in the saddle for hours and exhausted.

It was some small relief to know they'd be near other people soon. Maybe someone would see her and know she'd been taken against her will. Maybe she'd have a chance to get free.

They rode on a bit further and then she saw it.

A sizable hunting lodge in a clearing with a barn nearby, and a small cabin. A man stood on the porch with his hands on his hips, watching them ride in. Her hopes rose. Maybe this man would help her.

But as they rode nearer, her hopes crashed hard.

The man waiting was Mr. Henning Holland.

Her heart sunk. No one here was going to help her.

Mr. Holland stood scowling outside the hunting lodge as they rode up. "You're late," he said to Slade. "By an entire day."

Anger radiated off the man. Carolyn could hear it in his voice.

"Where have you been?" Holland demanded.

"Storm delayed us," Slade said. "We had to get her in, out of the rain, away from the lightning. Stopped at your line shack for shelter until it let up."

Henning Holland, still frowning, approached Carolyn, looking her up and down. "She's wet." His frown turned darker.

Carolyn shivered again, more from the look on his face than from how chilled she was.

"I told you to bring her here, unharmed." Anger laced his words and he seemed to be holding back a greater anger. "She could catch a chill and get sick." He waved his arm angrily. "Get her down off that horse. Now. And take that gag out."

The men hurried to comply and set her on the ground.

As soon as the gag was out, Carolyn tried to speak. Despite her dry tongue and mouth, she managed to croak out, "Kidnapping is against the law. You won't get away with this."

Her voice was not as strong as she wished. She needed water.

Henning Holland simply ignored her words as if she hadn't spoken, turned his back to her and stamped up the steps to his hunting lodge. He flung open the door. "Bertha!" he hollered.

Carolyn did not want to enter this lodge, or go anywhere near him, so she refused to move.

But Slade and the Mexican each took hold of one of her arms and pulled her up the stairs anyway, while the redhead led the horses away toward the barn. They pulled her through the open door.

Once she stepped inside the great room, she gasped.

On every wall hung dead animals, their heads stuffed, their shiny dead eyes staring right at her. It was a room of death and Mr. Holland was a killer.

"Ah. You see my collection," he said and swept his hand in a proud arc, taking in the entire room. "I shot all of them myself. Then had them mounted. As you can see, I'm quite an accomplished hunter."

Carolyn was used to men who hunted for food, not for trophies. They didn't boast about killing, they simply did what had to be done to feed their families.

"You're a killer," she said. He was proud of killing all these animals.

"I enjoy the hunt," he said. "And the kill. It takes great skill. Take this one," he pointed to a corner of the room where a large stuffed brown bear stood with teeth snarling and claws extended toward her. She shivered.

He frowned. "You distract me." He turned his head and bellowed. "Bertha!"

A short, heavy, gray haired woman hurried into the front room from the kitchen, wiping her hands on an apron.

"Miss Carolyn is here and she is chilled. Prepare a hot bath and make haste," Mr. Holland said to Bertha and then he turned to the two men who still stood on each side of her and roared, "Get out!"

Both men hurried back outside.

The moment the door closed behind them, Mr. Holland's tone and facial expression completely changed. "Now, my dear. Allow me to welcome you to my home away from home."

She stared at him, amazed at how quick he'd switched from angry to genial host, like a chameleon. This was the thing she had always sensed, even as a child. The genial face he put on with the townspeople was not how he really was. But even knowing it and seeing it confirmed, the speed with which he switched shook her. Goosebumps spread along her body.

"This is my hunting lodge, where I entertain guests. As my future wife, you will learn how I do things. We are only a bit less formal here than at my main house. I am a civilized hunter, a gentleman, not a ruffian." He smiled. "It is important to keep one's manners at all times."

"Gentlemen do not kidnap ladies," she said. "You are no gentleman."

He chuckled as if he found her amusing. "My dear, you are quite wrong. There are numerous tales of brides who were abducted by European aristocrats before their weddings. Brides who won't listen to reason cannot complain when the abduction happens. You have inflicted this upon yourself, which of course you cannot see, just yet. With time, you will see things my way."

"I will never see things your way."

He smiled without answering and then changed the subject. "This is the main room, and behind that door is the kitchen and the dining area. The other hallway leads to the bedrooms. Come," he said, as he placed his hand on her elbow. "I will show you to your room."

Her hands were still bound in front of her, but he

ignored that and acted as if this were a normal visit where he was showing her his home.

Everything was so strange. Surely this wasn't real. This couldn't be happening. She didn't know how to react, what to say or do. There was no one here to help her if she called out.

She was chilled more thoroughly than the rain had done, the chilling going all the way down to her bones and she stared at his hand and then at him as he moved her down the hallway.

Someone would have to untie her hands in order for her to take a bath, wouldn't they? Surely the woman named Bertha would see that she was here against her will.

Perhaps she'll help me get away, or get word to Mama of where I am. Then Matt will come.

Mr. Holland stopped outside of a door, turned the knob and then opened it.

The pink and white room inside was excessively feminine. It was the last thing she expected to find in Mr. Holland's hunting house. Pink and white wallpaper, pink lamps, pink and white curtains over a darkened window and an ornate brass bed against one wall. The fireplace, on the other wall, held a warm and cheerful fire. Carolyn had never seen suck a delicate and feminine room, and she would have loved it, had the house belonged to anyone else. But because it was past of Mr. Holland's house, she hated the room. Every delicate piece and part of it.

Bertha looked up at them from where she stirred hot water into a tub. Beside her was a set of perfumed soap with several bars to choose from, a thick towel to dry off with and a fancy brush and comb set. A white dressing gown embroidered with pink flowers lay across a chair.

"Bertha," he said. "I've brought your charge. You know what to do."

Carolyn tried to make eye contact with the older woman, but she was only focused on Mr. Holland. In his employ it was likely how she kept her job.

"Yes sir," Bertha said.

Glancing down at her tied hands, Carolyn held them out. "Cut me loose," she said.

It wasn't a request.

Holland smiled at her as if they were exchanging pleasantries. "Of course, my dear." He winked at her. "Whatever you request."

"In that case," she began, but he cut her off.

"As long as I approve of your request," he said.

"Let me go." She begged. "Please. Let me go."

"Marry me," he said. "Then I will allow you to do whatever you wish. Within reason."

She shook her head. "No."

"This will be your room," he spoke, as if she hadn't answered him. "As you can see, I've spared no expense to make your room perfect. You have the finest linens, French soaps, all the things a lady might require."

"You decorated a whole room for me? How long have you been planning this?"

"To marry you? Since you were quite young."

Her jaw dropped.

"But your mother and father didn't believe in child marriages so I had to wait."

Her eyes widened in horror.

She hadn't been crazy, or imagining things, when she'd sensed something behind his watching her.

He'd just admitted what she'd felt even when she was too young to understand.

Stepping in front of her, he bent to untie her hands. "I have men guarding the house to keep you safe. This was not necessary. And that gag," He shook his head. "I fear my men were unnecessarily rough with you." He took hold of her hands in his, massaging her wrists where red marks from where the rope had rubbed had left her skin sore and red.

She flinched.

He held her hands firm and still and gazed into her eyes. "Tell me. Did they touch you?"

Remembering the way the Mexican had wanted to had her glancing away.

Holland squeezed her hands, his voice changing again. "I realize this is a delicate question, but I must know. Did they touch you, take liberties with you?"

"The leader checked me for guns."

"That fool." His grip tightened and she winced again. "I told him you would not have a gun. He checked beneath your clothes? His hands were on your skin?"

"No. On top of my clothes."

"Where did he touch you? Your breasts?" Holland was beginning to breathe heavily as he looked down at her breasts.

"No, not there. My skirt. My legs."

"Between your legs?" He had a strange light in his eyes as they searched hers, looking for something.

"No, not there."

"No one has touched you there?"

"No." She hated telling him, but knew he wanted a virgin. It was a good thing she was. God only knew what he'd do to her if he thought she wasn't.

Her purity gave her a level of safety from him. For now.

His face changed again, back to that of a smooth gentleman. "Good. You will remain my virgin bride, safe within these walls until our wedding night. Bertha will look after you now. Enjoy your bath. Get warm. I won't have you getting sick."

She didn't answer him, but remained silent as he left and closed the door.

Click. She jumped and jerked her head toward the door. *He locked me in!*

Bertha came over to her and helped her out of her wet clothing as if nothing was amiss. As if it were perfectly normal for him to be locking the door, imprisoning them both.

"Step in," she said, "Your hands are like ice."

"I am cold," Carolyn admitted as she stepped into the warm bath.

Slipping down into the water felt good. Her feet had grown so chilled she couldn't feel her toes so the warm water was a shock at first, but soon she was laying back in the tub, having her hair washed by Bertha's capable hands. Trying to forget the horrible circumstances of her kidnapping, as part of her mind wanted to do that, to escape in a different way. But she was unable to.

"Bertha?" she asked, keeping her eyes closed and her tone innocent.

"Yes, miss?"

"You know those men brought me here against my will. I don't want to be here. I want to go home to my mother, where I belong. You see papa just died, and mama needs me."

Bertha's hands stilled. She was listening.

Perhaps she will help me to go. To get away from from Mr. Holland.

"I am sorry about your father." Bertha said and then her

hands began to move again, massaging Carolyn's head. "It is hard to lose them."

'Yes, it is. So you can see why I cannot stay here."

"I will ask Mr. Holland if your mother can visit you soon. He is a good man. I am sure he will understand that you miss your mother."

"No, I can't stay here. This is kidnapping, Bertha. You saw how they brought me in. He sent men to take me right as I was feeding the animals. Mama doesn't even know where I am. I wasn't there to call her to supper. She doesn't eat unless I remind her. Papa hasn't been gone long. And for me to just disappear? Mama must be worried sick."

Bertha frowned. "That is not like Mr. Holland. He should not have done that. Your poor mother. I will ask him to send her a message as soon as possible, so she will not worry."

"You don't seem to understand what I'm trying to tell you. I can't stay here. I must go home. Now."

"Well, you will have to discuss that over dinner tonight with Mr. Holland. I'm sure you can work something out." She beamed a big smile. "He's doted on you since you were a child. And he's done so much to prepare this room for you, to get everything ready to welcome you into his life. We're very excited to soon have a lady Holland to preside over his dinner parties, much as his mother used to back east. Now close your eyes for the rinse water."

Carolyn closed her eyes, the unreality of everything washing over her as Bertha lifted a pitcher of water and slowly rinsed Carolyn's long blonde hair.

When Bertha was done, Carolyn spoke again. "You knew his mother?"

"Oh yes. I have been serving the Holland family since Henning was a baby boy. Used to bathe him too. He's done well for himself. Mr. Holland is a generous man. You will want for nothing. You will do fine. But, you must remember one important thing." She bent near Carolyn's ear and whispered into it as she glanced back at the doorknob. "You must never, ever criticize him, even a little bit, even in jest. His temper will not be controllable if you do and even I cannot predict what he would do then. You, my dear, must learn to be agreeable."

"Agreeable?" Carolyn sputtered.

Bertha placed one hand on each side of Carolyn's face. "Listen to me, child. Henning will be kind and generous with you, but you must not anger him. That would not be safe."

Wide eyed and wondering just what kind of a monster Henning really was, beyond what she already knew, Carolyn sat frozen in the warm bathtub, chills running across her shoulders and arms, raising goose bumps again.

"Out, now. You mustn't catch a chill," Bertha's eyes showed fear, as she hurried her charge up and out of the tub, while reaching for the towel.

It was clear she was afraid of Mr. Holland's reaction to Carolyn catching a chill.

CHAPTER 6

*M*r. Holland came in just as Bertha was tying the back of Carolyn's corset.

The newest fashions in dresses required a low, tiny waist and a full, low bust supported by a corset and then a bustle in the back, instead of the looser, simple country dresses that Carolyn and her mother wore on the ranch.

With one knock on the door, he then flung the door open and there he was, glass of whiskey in his hand, and dressed as if for a night out on the town.

"Mr. Holland!" Carolyn gasped and moved her hands to cover herself. All of her new underthings were white and thin enough to see through. She kept one hand down below to cover the patch of hair he might see through the thin with fabric and with her other hand and arm she attempted to cover her breasts.

"I trust that warm bath did you good," he spoke, as if she weren't standing before him, half naked. "It appears to have restored a healthy pink to your face and limbs."

That healthy pink was climbing up her cheeks as her embarrassment grew. "Sir, I am not properly dressed."

"No you are not," he agreed. "But you are a lovely sight to behold." He strode to the tall wooden wardrobe and flung open the doors. "Now," he said. "Look at all the beautiful dresses I have here for you. All for you, my dear."

He reached in and plucked out a soft blue dress, and then turned to show it to her. "You will wear this one tonight. Dinner is promptly at six. I will return for you then. You rest now. There are dark circles under your eyes."

He turned toward Bertha. "Loosen that corset so she can breathe. And make sure she takes a restorative nap. I won't have her dozing off at dinner. She may wear her hair down tonight as we discussed."

There seemed to be little choice in the matter, and Carolyn was truly exhausted, after being awake all night and the stress of being abducted. The heated water in the tub had helped her aching muscles to relax and she now she had to admit she was incredibly sleepy. She yawned. She didn't really want to sleep, but she yawned.

"I will come for you promptly at six," he said. "Be ready."

Ready.

She needed to be ready to escape. She yawned again. Her body needed sleep. If she rested she'd be ready to escape at the first opportunity. She needed to be ready.

With a nod to her, he was out the door again and she heard the lock click.

Locked in again.

Bertha loosened the corset. "Into bed with you," she said.

Carolyn yawned again. *So tired. Tomorrow I will see about getting away. Right now I need sleep and later, food.*

Bertha sat in a rocker in the room, rocking and mending a shirt as she watched over Carolyn.

My maid, as if I were a child, Carolyn thought. *But really another one of my jailors.* That was the last thought she had before she fell asleep.

She slept for a while and didn't hear Bertha leave the room.

But later she heard the door open and woke. Though tired and somewhat groggy, she realized that Bertha had left and was coming back into the room.

Which meant either Mr. Holland had let Bertha out, or, Bertha had a key. And if she had a key, Carolyn might be able to get that key.

"I hope you slept well, dear," Bertha said. "Time to get up now and dress for dinner."

"I did," Carolyn said. She sat up in bed and stretched, trying to lose the groggy feeling. She needed to be sharp witted for this dinner. She had to convince Holland to let her go home again.

Her stomach growled, it had been so long since she'd eaten.

"My goodness, you must be very hungry," Bertha said. "It's a fine feast the master has planned for you tonight. He knows all your favorites."

"How could he possibly know that?"

"I don't know how he learns all the things he does, but he's a very smart man."

Likely, since he'd been watching her since she was a child, he'd been taking notes of every little thing she did. Everything she liked. The thought of him studying her for so long and thinking of marrying her, before she was even old enough to know what that might entail made her skin crawl.

She let Bertha help her dress and then comb her hair again. Soon she was ready.

The knock came at the door at five minutes before six. One knock and then the door opened.

Now he knocks. But waits for no one to respond or open the door.

Then she realized he hadn't unlocked the door. Was there a pattern or had that been a mistake? Could she rush out the door while Bertha was inside and thought she was sleeping?

I must think and find a way out. One that would work. Before Bertha and Mr. Holland suspect I will run.

"Promptly ready," he said. "I am pleased. And you, my dear, look lovely tonight. That shade of blue against your skin and hair is lovely, just lovely." He smiled and held out his hand. "Come. I'll escort you to dinner."

Escort like a prisoner, Carolyn thought, as she stepped forward, determined that this would be her last meal with him. Her stomach growled again.

"You're undoubtedly hungry," he said. "I know they did not feed you. They were supposed to deliver much sooner and I apologize for the delay. But now we shall rectify that with the delicious cooking of Bertha and George."

How could Bertha have cooked dinner and also watched over me? Carolyn wondered with a frown. "Bertha seems a woman of many talents," she said.

"They are both treasures," he said. "Been with my family for years. Bertha was my nursemaid and is now my cook and her husband George is my butler, but also an excellent cook. He has grilled our finest steaks to perfection."

Her stomach growled again at the very thought of a tender, juicy, Texas steak.

"And wait til you taste Bertha's apple pie," he said. "But you will find out for yourself soon enough."

They entered the dining room, a dark room with heavy, wooden furniture but lit by a large candelabrum in the center of the table, which was set with fine china and crystal. For two.

He walked her to her chair and then released her hand. The butler pulled out the chair for her and she sat. Mr. Holland walked around to the other side of the table and was seated. The butler then came back to where Carolyn was seated and placed a cloth napkin onto her lap. Then he walked to the other side of the table and did the same thing for Mr. Holland. Then he said, "Wine, sir?"

"Yes," Mr. Holland said. "You may pour."

The butler poured his wine and then came to Carolyn's side and poured her a glass.

Oh dear, she thought. *If we have to wait for the butler to do everything, this is going to be a very long meal and a very long evening.*

She had never dined in such a formal fashion before.

"I realize you may not be used to the formalities, growing up on that ranch," he said. "You are a simple country girl."

Her eyes narrowed. "If I'm so simple, don't you see that I'm the wrong woman for you to marry?" She gestured to the table. "This is far beyond what I am used to. I'd not be a good choice to preside at your fancy evening events."

"On the contrary, my dear," he said with a laugh. "The best bride is one who is easily trained and has no previous bad habits needing correction."

She snorted. "If you think I am easily trained, you do not know me at all. Which is my point. You have chosen the wrong woman."

"I shall enjoy training you," he said. "This is how we shall dine every evening. Tonight, because I know how hungry you must be, and it is just the two of us, I will allow you to eat as much and as quickly as you want. Within reason."

"Allow me?" her voice rose.

"Tomorrow I must attend to business in town and will not be dining with you, but we will begin after that."

He merely smiled and nodded to the butler to bring the first course.

"Gazpacho soup," the butler announced. Then he dished a serving out into Carolyn's soup bowl and placed a soupspoon beside her.

Being so hungry her stomach was actually starting to hurt, she reached for her spoon before Mr. Holland had his soup. She didn't care if she was being rude.

MATT AND JAKE followed the tracks until they found a line shack up ahead. They approached carefully in case someone was inside. But the shack was empty.

They nosed about inside and outside the shack and noted from the tracks that a party had stayed there recently.

"Likely they stopped over here," Jake said. "Probably taking shelter from that same storm that moved through the other night."

Matt nodded. "Likely. We need to get a move on."

Jake followed Matt this time, letting him take the lead. After a few hours, he shouted "Hold up."

Matt reined in beside him. "What?"

Jake searched Matt's face. "You got a good handle on their trail?"

"Sure," Matt said.

"I don't see it," Jake said.

"Damn it," Matt cursed and got down off his horse. He began looking around for signs.

Jake looked too and found nothing. "Looks like we've lost their trail."

"Damn," Matt cursed again. He took off his hat and waved it forward. "If we keep going in that direction," he said. "We'll pick it up again. We know that's the direction they're headed."

"How?" Jake asked.

"You know men usually travel in a straight line to where they're headed." Matt said. "Now come on, we're wasting time."

"It's no good Matt," Jake shook his head. "We need to go back to where you last saw their trail and pick it up from there."

Matt got a strange look on his face and Jake had a bad feeling about this.

"Daylight is wasting," Matt said.

"Tell you what. You go on and follow whatever it is you're following. I'm going back to pick up that trail. If I have to go all the way back to the shack to do it." He got back on his horse and turned his horse around.

Muttering, Matt got back on his horse. Though his mood was dark, he followed Jake.

After circling back to where they'd started, Jake's suspicion turned out to be true. Matt had followed the direction he'd thought they went. He hadn't been tracking. He was too worried about his sister to be thinking clearly.

With much difficulty, Jake found the trail again. And the trail led in a different direction.

They had now wasted another day, due to Matt's rash charge ahead mindset. Even Matt now realized he was too emotional to be making the decisions this time.

Jake was now in charge until they found Carolyn. Matt needed Jakes clear headed, slow methodical skills to find them. They rode until darkness prevented them from seeing the trail, but they had already wasted another day and the knowledge was bitter to both men.

They didn't speak to each other for the rest of the evening.

∼

THE NEXT DAY Matt and Jake were up before the sun rose and mounted the moment they could see to track again.

"We know which way they were headed. We should be able to catch up with them faster now," Jake said.

Matt grunted. He was still mad at himself for being so rash.

The horses were refreshed, so they rode hard to make up for time. It had already been four days since they'd learned she'd been taken.

Just before noon, as they rode over a ridge, Jake saw smoke rising down in a valley from a small settlement. "Buildings up ahead. You know who lives here?"

"Was the Johnson place, but I didn't know of anyone living on this part of it."

"You sure? You've only been gone two years."

"They must've built all this quickly."

A long large ranch style house dominated the landscape. There was a barn nearby and a cabin with scattered smaller buildings.

"This is the direction they were coming. Do you think she's here?" Matt said.

"If she's not here, they rode through, because this is where their tracks lead," Jake said. "Let's go down and see.

You still don't need to be recognized. You let me do the talking."

Matt was already glaring.

Jake didn't need Matt's temper to get in the way. "We don't know what the situation is down there. You've got to keep a cool head."

Matt looked like he'd like to hit someone, but Jake knew he'd listen to reason and trust his partner.

They rode down into the valley toward the main house.

"Do you see the redhead with the gun, sitting on that tree stump?" Matt said.

A redheaded man jumped up, startled, and picked up his gun.

"Yeah I saw him. I didn't see any others," Jake said. "But someone's in that house."

"She must be in there, in the main house," Matt said. "I don't know whose house this is. Johnsons could never afford this."

"Poker face," Jake reminded him, knowing this was hard for Matt and his facial expression right now would give him away.

"Hello," Jake called to the redhead. "Permission to enter the camp."

"Who are you? What do you want?" the red head said.

"Texas Rangers, traveling through."

The minute the redhead heard Texas Rangers, his eyes widened and his face turned pale beneath his freckles.

It wasn't wise to take unkindly to a Texas Ranger. A Ranger carried more clout with him than a sheriff. A ranger's jurisdiction for law and bringing justice ranged farther and he often acted as jailor, judge and executioner. Even good law abiding citizens were afraid of the rangers.

"How can I help you?" he said.

"One of our horses got a rock in his shoe. Wondering if you have any smithy tools," Jake said.

"There's a stable, but I don't know what tools we got. Let me go talk to my boss," he said, looking as if he couldn't wait to get away from them. Then he hurried into the house to find his boss.

"Hey Slade," they heard him call.

They waited patiently.

A man dressed all in black came out onto the porch and then down the steps. "Texas Rangers, you say?"

"Yes. We're Rangers." Jake showed his badge. "Travelling through. One of our horses got a stone in his foot and we were wondering if you had any tools."

"I don't know but you can go look," Slade said.

"It's getting late in the day. You have a place where we can sleep tonight?" Jake asked.

"You can bed down in the barn, with your horses. More than what you're used to. Roof over your head instead of the sky," Slade said.

"True. Thank you kindly." Jake smiled and nodded.

"Eli here will show you where the stables are," Slade nodded toward the younger man with the read hair.

Jake tipped his hat. "Much obliged."

"You're welcome," the man said.

They turned and Jake felt the man's glare, before briefly turning his head just enough to see it out of the corner of his eye.

He was a man who was hiding something in his past. Possibly more than one thing. A man who already viewed Texas Rangers as his enemies.

Jake and Matt dismounted and followed Eli to the stables.

"Wherever you want to bed down is up to you," Eli said.

"The tack room is over there. That's where the tools would be, if we got em. You can figure it out. Come find me if you need anything." He didn't wait for an answer but hurried away as quick as he could.

"Wonder if he's always this nervous," Jake said. He reached down and picked up one of his horse's hooves to inspect it. "Sure are a lot of new people around here. Nobody knows where anything is. If that kid's boss was the foreman, he'd know where everything was around here."

Matt nodded in agreement. "I'll see what they've got." He went into the tool room to see what was there. He came back and said, "It's well stocked and everything is new. But they don't know what they've got."

Jake said. "These guys aren't ranch hands. Slade's a gunman if I've ever seen one. Neither of them look like cow punchers."

Matt replied. "There are four horses. Same as we tracked."

"Yes," Jake said. "We need to find out who is in main the house."

"I want to know who owns all this. They've spared no expense. None of this was here two years ago," Matt said.

"Someone is coming," Jake said.

Matt hushed immediately.

"Amigos amigos," a short, stocky Mexican called out as he entered the barn. "Hola. How are you? Mr. Slade, he said you were out here. How is your horse?"

"We think he got a small stone," Jake said. "It's out now. Once he's rested, he'll be fine tomorrow."

"Bueno. That is good." The Mexican nodded, smiling. He moved to feed and water the four horses in the barn, still smiling. He whistled as he fed and watered them.

"The grandma, in the house, she makes good cornbread

and frijoles. I can bring you some. You like it caliente? Hot?" the Mexican said.

"Hot is good," Jake said.

"Si, it is very good," the Mexican said. Once he'd finished feeding and watering the horses, he left the barn.

After he left, Jake said, "None of them introduced themselves."

"I noticed that," Matt said. "Not your typical citizens."

Jake gave him a nod that meant they were thinking the same thing, without having to say much about it. Citizens tended to introduce themselves. Outlaws and gunmen, people breaking the laws of the land, did not. Especially to rangers who often knew the names of wanted men and went in search of them. If the younger man hadn't called for Slade, they wouldn't know his name. Of course neither of the rangers had given their names either, because Matt didn't want his name getting around.

The Mexican came back carrying two plates of hot food for them. "Now you will enjoy," he said. "The grandmother cooks as good as my mother in Mexico."

"Thank you," Jake said, taking a plate. "What brought you up this way?"

"Good work and good pay," he said. "My mother is dead many years and my father before her. This is my home now."

Matt took the plate from the Mexican and mumbled, "Thank you."

"He speaks," the Mexican said.

Matt took a bite and nodded. "Mm," he said.

"This is very good," Jake said. "Tell the grandmother we said so and thank you for the meal."

"You are welcome. I will tell her. Leave the plates there when you are done." He pointed to a bale of hay.

"We will," Jake said.

"I will leave you to eat," the man nodded and left the barn again.

Jake waited several minutes before saying real low, "He must be the foreman here. Yet Slade was the boss the boy called for."

"Boss in charge of what?" Matt asked.

"That's right. In charge of what." Jake said.

Soon the Mexican came back for the empty plates. It was getting close to dark and he'd just turned to leave when a buggy and horse came into the yard. "The owner is here," he said, placing plates back down again and giving them a quick nod before hurrying out the barn door toward the buggy.

"Now, we'll see the owner I expect," Jake said.

They both moved to where they could look out but not be seen. The buggy stopped and a man stepped down from it. As they observed, the Mexican walked up to the man and took the reins of the buggy from him.

Matt cursed low.

Jake knew before asking but he asked anyway. "Holland?"

"Yeah." Matt's hands were fisted, his anger rising.

Jake clapped a hand on his shoulder. "Patience," he said.

Matt was not known for his patience. He would blow if Jake weren't here.

"Jose," Holland said, his good mood apparent from his tone. "I'm staying overnight. My bags are in back. Bring them to my room."

"Yes sir," Jose said, with a nod.

Holland walked to the front door as Jose took the bags out of the back of the buggy and around to the back of the house.

Matt's face was filled with fury. "She's in there," he said. "I knew Holland was behind this."

"Tonight," Jake said. "We'll wait til they're asleep. We'd best move back. Put the bedrolls out and prepare, but act normal."

That meant, keep their guns handy even as they slept at night. It was nothing they hadn't done many times before.

BERTHA WAS in Carolyn's room, helping her dress, when Carolyn heard the front door close and footsteps in the main room.

"Slade," Mr. Holland said. "Looks like you'll get your bonus. You've done well. Nobody knows the girl is missing. Her mother hasn't been to town."

Carolyn could hear the satisfaction in his voice. *He thinks he's getting away with this! But he doesn't know that mama doesn't need to go to town with Matt and Jake handling things.*

"Mr. Holland," Slade said. "That is good news. Thank you."

"I'll pay you this Friday. Now I have dinner with my lovely bride to be to prepare for."

"Before I go out to the bunk house, there is one thing you need to know," Slade said. "We have a couple of Texas Rangers in the barn, sleeping overnight."

Carolyn caught her breath. *Rangers? That meant Matt and Jake were here.*

"Rangers?" Holland's voice rose. "What the hell are they doing here?"

"They had horse trouble."

"Make *sure* they leave in the morning," Holland growled. "Now I need to go check on my bride."

She heard the front door open and close. *Slade must have left.*

Footsteps moved down the hall. She heard another door open and close and Holland clearing his throat. As if he had something in it. More footsteps and then he knocked once on her door and opened it.

Bertha had finished fussing with Carolyn's hair, which was pulled up, soft tendrils falling down beside her neck and curling slightly.

Holland's gaze took her in and he cleared his throat again. "You are a vision of loveliness, my dear. And, ready for dinner ahead of time! Excellent, Bertha. You may go prepare dinner."

Bertha nodded and scurried out of the room.

It must be a lot on the older woman to have to play ladies maid and also be the cook here. This situation had to seem unusual to her.

"This situation is not proper," Carolyn said. "When are you going to let me go?"

CHAPTER 7

*M*r. Holland did not answer her. He showed no response at all, as if he was preoccupied with something on his mind, and hadn't heard her.

"Well?," she said.

Hearing Carolyn's voice, he snapped out of it.

"Sorry my dear. I was thinking of business when I should have been thinking of you. The work day is over and you have my full attention now." He smiled at her.

She couldn't let on that she knew the two rangers. "Oh that's quite all right," she said. "I know you're a businessman with many interests. I was hoping you would tell me more about them at dinner."

His face brightened. "Of course, of course." Taking her by the elbow he said, "Come along to the parlor with me, my dear. We will enjoy a glass of wine before dinner is served."

He ushered her into the parlor and then she watched him pour her a glass of wine. He poured himself a glass and took a large swallow.

Had knowing there were rangers on the property made him nervous?

She didn't want him thinking about the rangers. "I do believe this dress needs to be taken in a bit," she said, glancing down at her cleavage where this dress was a bit looser than the others. "Bertha thought so too, but I wanted to wear the deeper blue tonight."

She took a sip of her wine and watched him over the rim of the glass.

His gaze went to the skin showing where the neckline of her dress ended. "The deep blue velvet is even more becoming on you than the lighter blue dress. And the neckline is fine the way it is," he said. "You may fill it out more with a few more good meals."

"I was wondering," she began. He waited patiently for her to finish. "This is a large hunting lodge and you also have that big house. How many properties do you own?"

"Oh several," he said, and then began to list them.

Smiling and nodding pretending to be fascinated, she waited until he was finished and then said, "And the land? How many acres do you have?"

He listed his acreage, and then said, "After we are married, all my properties will be yours as well. Your mother could even live closer and not be all-alone in that big ranch which she'll never be able to keep going by herself. She can stay on our properties and well and there are servants to help. You have not perhaps considered what a burden running a ranch would be for a widowed woman."

She continued on. "How many horses do you have and how many herds of cattle?"

He listed them and then said, "You can select a horse of your own. One that is broken and suitable for a lady, of course." He smiled at her. "You are a fetching figure atop a horse, but you won't be riding the fields, or working with the horses. I have plenty of men to do that. You can learn to ride like a lady, with a proper riding habit and gloves."

A plate crashed in the kitchen and Bertha exclaimed, "Oh no, George you must be more careful!"

Holland rose. "Excuse me." He hurried from the parlor to the kitchen.

It was the first time he'd left her alone outside of her locked room. She hurried to the window to look out, peering through the curtains and hoping to see Matt or Jake and for one of them to see her. Was there a way to signal to them that she was in here?

"What happened here?" Holland barked out at the elderly couple.

"I'm so sorry master Holland," George said.

"That was irreplaceable china my family brought over from Germany," Holland said. "Which you know."

She could hear the anger in his voice and the quick switch from his charming good mood to this anger was frightening.

No, there was no one outside the window that she could see. Then Slade rounded the corner on front of the house and Carolyn pulled back quickly, letting the curtains fall again. She rushed back to her seat.

"I apologize, sir," George said. "It won't happen again."

"See that it doesn't. Or I will be replacing you, not my china," Holland said.

Holland came back into the parlor, suddenly pleasant again. "Sorry you had to hear that." He glanced at his clock. "Dinner is late." He forced a smile, which did not reach his eyes, and she could see that he was still angry about the plate.

George announced dinner.

Holland rose and held out his hand. "Shall we?" He waited for her to put her hand in his and then he escorted her into the dining room.

George brought out a roast on what must've been another clean plate and placed it on the table. He sliced off a piece and put it on Carolyn's plate and then did the same for Holland. Then he went back to the kitchen and brought out a bowl of vegetables.

They made it through the meal without any more accidents or outbursts and as Carolyn kept asking questions and showing interest in all of Holland's possessions, he was more than happy to boast about it all.

Finally as they were having dessert, he said, "Now my dear, do you see the benefits to marrying me? As you can see you will want for nothing and you will have a husband who dotes on you. Marry me."

She laid her fork down, focused on the napkin in her lap and gathered everything she had to utter her next words. "I, I will think about it."

His eyes widened in surprise, clearly expecting to have to keep pushing her to marry him and not expecting such a quick and positive response. "My dear," she began to speak with a smile. "I am so glad to hear this. Yes, yes. Do think about it."

She gathered her napkin and placed it on her plate, having had enough of this and not knowing how much longer she could keep it up. "And now, I am quite tired and wish to retire to my room for the evening."

She was quite tired of him and of being in his house and these long, tedious dinners.

He made as if to push back from his chair and she said, "No need to hurry. I know the way. You can stay and finish your dessert."

Surprised, he looked at his plate and the last few bites of pie and said, "Yes, you may be excused and I shall see you in the morning, before I leave for my office in town."

"Thank you. Good night."

"Good night, my dear," he said.

She walked out of the dining room and eyed the great front room where the front door was, wishing she could make a run for it. But, she heard his chair push back and knew he could easily run after her and catch her again. She needed to keep playing along.

Walking down the hall to her room, she felt as if he were watching. She opened the door and stepped inside, closing it behind her. Now if they would just not lock her in.

But she heard the footsteps and then the click of the key in the lock. Bertha would come in soon and help her to undress. Maybe she would leave the door unlocked when she left or maybe she would get a message to the rangers in the barn.

When Bertha came to help her undress, Carolyn said, "I'm terribly tired and need a good nights sleep tonight. Please don't come in to disturb me this evening."

"Of course, miss," Bertha said, helping her to remove the heavy blue velvet dress.

As soon as Carolyn was in her nightgown, she slipped into bed and pulled the covers up. "Good night, Bertha," she said.

"Good night, miss," Bertha said. She let the room and after closing the door, locked it.

This time, Carolyn was glad the door was locked. She would use that to her advantage. Slipping back out of bed, she went over to the wardrobe and found some practical riding clothes and boots. She put them on, ready to run at a moments notice.

~

MATT AND JAKE kept watch on the house and left their bedrolls open to hurry into if they needed to.

Everyone was asleep, in the house and in the bunkhouse, they assumed when all the lights were out and enough time had passed with no sounds other than the occasional hoot owl. They slipped out of the barn and moved through the shadows.

Eli was on guard duty but lazy as he was, he hadn't moved from his post and was now dozing off.

Matt quickly knocked him out, hitting the back of his head.

Jake helped Matt to tie the boy up and then they left him behind a tree where the others wouldn't see him.

They moved on toward the back door of the large house, prepared to sneak in, find Carolyn and get her out without anyone knowing.

Jake believed this was the best plan, the safest plan for Carolyn.

Just as Matt opened the back door for them to head inside, an older heavyset man wearing a robe was coming toward the door, likely heading out to the outhouse. They startled him.

He jumped. "What are you doing here?" he yelled and grabbed the door, slamming it.

Matt took a shot at him, but missed.

So much for a quiet rescue, Jake thought, drawing his gun as Matt shot at the man.

Both of them charged into the room, guns drawn. Seeing the man reach for a rifle, Matt shot again, this time hitting the man in the leg.

The man cried out, gripping his leg, and falling to the floor.

"Where's the girl?" Jake yelled at the man.

"Where's Holland?" Matt yelled.

An old woman ran into the kitchen. "George? Mine Got!" She lapsed into German and the two of them spoke quickly to each other.

Guns still drawn and pointed at the old couple, Jake gestured for them to move away. "Stay out of our way," Jake commanded.

She nodded, frantic, and pulled at her husband to get him to move into the other room, her eyes wide with fear. Once through the door, she called back to them, "Don't hurt the girl."

Brave behind doors like most citizens, he thought with a half grin and a shake of his head.

They moved toward the main room, guns drawn, and just as they entered, the front door burst open and Slade and Jose entered, their guns drawn.

"Texas Rangers," Jake called, knowing it wouldn't stop these men.

Usually one to follow laws and practices of a good lawman, who worked with citizens and the courts, no one could say he didn't warn people before he shot them. Though often he had to call out and shoot at the same time.

Slade shot as he charged into the room at the same time Jake called the words out and fired along with Matt.

Matt's shot, hit Slade square in the chest, knocking him back against the wall and he slid down.

Slade's shot hit Jake, grazing his arm and he jerked, his shot hitting Jose in the arm.

Jose dove behind a long couch and called out. "No mas," he said. "No more. I've been shot in my arm. I give up."

Slade wasn't speaking any time soon.

"Are you all right?" Matt asked Jake.

"I'm okay," Jake said. "He just grazed me. I'm going to look for Carolyn." He ran down the hallway in the direction he thought she was.

Carolyn was screaming at Holland from that direction.

CAROLYN HAD BEEN SITTING on the pink velvet seat of her dressing table where she'd leaned her elbow and propped her head up on her hand. Her head was bobbing, and she was in that hard to stay awake yet not wanting to get into bed to sleep mode when she heard what sounded like a gunshot.

What's going on? That was a gunshot!

She leapt up and ran to the door. Tested the doorknob. It was still locked. But she was dressed and ready to run. She ran to the window even though she could not see out past the boarded up window and she heard another shot fired.

Two gunshots. But who is shooting? And at who? I hope Matt and Jake are coming for me.

Desperate to be away from the fancy bedroom and away from Holland, Carolyn tried to think of what she could do to get out of the room, or to let them know where she was, without bringing Holland or his men here to guard against her getting away. Her mind raced with worry and frustration. She couldn't get out and she couldn't see what was going on.

Then the key turned in the lock and Holland stepped into the room.

"You're dressed and ready," Holland said, pleased surprise in his eyes. "Good girl." He hurried over to her. As he drew near she could see money and deeds stuck into his bag along with the ivory handle of a silver gun. "They're here to steal my land," he said, reaching for her hand. "We need to go. Now."

She yanked her hand back, away from him. "I didn't do this for you," she yelled. "That Texas ranger is my brother. They've come for me."

"He's dead." Holland reached for her again, grabbing her wrist this time.

"No he's not. He's here. Let me go." She jerked her hand hard, trying to pull her wrist loose from his tight grip.

"Never. You are mine."

"I'm not." She tried twisting her arm back and forth and broke loose.

"You're coming with me," Holland reached for her again, but she ran to the corner of the room, trying to get around and past him, to make it out that door.

"Matt!" She screamed.

"Texas Rangers," Jake yelled, from the other side of the door.

"Help!" Carolyn called.

He kicked the door, knocking it open and entered, with both guns drawn. The most fearsome and strong sight, Carolyn had ever seen. Her heart leapt. Jake was here!

In Holland's last lunge for her, he was distracted by Jakes appearance in the doorway.

"Jake," Carolyn gasped out. "Where's Matt?"

Jake looked at her. "He's fine."

Holland reached into his bag to draw his gun and Carolyn, seeing and knowing he had a gun, screamed.

But Jake fired off a shot before Holland could fully draw and fire.

With deadly aim and a calm steady hand, Jake killed Holland with one shot to the center of his forehead.

Blood and brain splattered all over the feminine pink and white wallpaper.

Carolyn gasped. And then, taking another deep breath she cried out. "Oh Jake." Running to him now, her arms outreached, she wanted him to hold her.

Jake caught her in one arm, holding his gun away from her.

She wrapped her arms around his neck and held on tight, so relieved she was to be safe and rescued by Jake. He'd take her out and away from this horrible pink room and that horrible man. He'd take her to her brother.

"You're safe now," he said, holstering one gun. The other a precaution. He gave her a quick squeeze and then let go. "I want you to stay behind me," he said. "Just until we know the dust has settled."

She let go of him and went to move behind him when she noticed the blood on his sleeve. "Oh, no. Jake, you're hurt," she said, moving closer again to look at his wound.

"It's nothing. Stay behind me now."

"All right," She moved behind him with a frown.

"Come on, and stay close," he moved out of the room and back down the hall toward the front room.

Slade now sat, eyes open, but unseeing against one wall of the room. He was dead in a pool of blood.

Carolyn looked around the room. The dead animals stared back at her. She'd felt from the first time she'd entered this room that it was a room of death.

The Mexican moaned. "Help me. I'm shot." He sat holding his leg. His shirt was off and tied around his thigh, to slow the bleeding.

Matt came into the room. "All clear in the house," he said to Jake. "The old man needs patched up."

Jake nodded.

"Oh Matt," Carolyn ran to Matt, so happy to see him again. "I knew you'd come for me," she said. "I knew you'd find me."

Guns holstered now, he hugged her. "I'm glad you're safe, little sister. We're gonna take you home."

Jake could have sworn he saw the man tearing up.

After a few touching moments, the siblings let go of each other.

"I'm ready to go," Carolyn said. "I can't wait to be home and to let mama know that I'm all right. And see Dash again."

Matt and Jake exchanged glances.

"Please. My George, he is hurt," Bertha said. She had come into the room while they were talking. "He needs a doctor."

"We'll have to take the wounded into town to see the doc before we can take you home and we need to drop that one at the jail and take the bodies to the morgue. But I'll have the sheriff send someone to tell mama that you're safe and coming home."

"I just don't want to worry her any more than she has been," Carolyn said.

"It's an hour and a half to town," Matt said. "We'll head there in the morning and send a man right away."

"KID LOAD the horses and the buggy," Matt said to Eli. The sun was just rising and they'd all had coffee. "Put the bodies on horses. George and Bertha can ride in the buggy and Jose will drive it. Everyone else will be on horseback."

The kid wasn't fast, but everyone co-operated. Jose drove while Bertha fussed over George in the back of the buggy. Jake and Matt rode their horses and Carolyn rode one of Mr. Holland's. The two horses carrying the bodies of Holland and Slade came along behind the buggy with Eli riding alongside to make sure they didn't fall off. Since he'd been the one to load them, Matt assigned him that task.

There were quite a sight riding into town and citizens and shopkeepers stopped to look and see it. Everyone knew the sight of Mr. Holland's buggy, and the whispers started immediately. A boy in the street ran ahead, straight for the sheriff's office. Matt and Jake knew the sheriff would have heard before they ever reached the sheriffs office.

Carolyn, however, was not used to the stares and whispers. "This is what they did after papa was killed," she told Matt who was riding on her left side. "Whispering around him at the funeral like old flies."

"I know you hate it," Jake said, "But those whispers may have helped save you. Everyone thought Matt was dead, including Holland."

"Some still think that," she said.

"They'll soon learn I am very much alive," Matt said. "You and mama have nothing to worry about any more."

"Does that mean you are staying?" Her voice was hopeful.

"Yes," he said. "I am staying. But you let me tell mama."

"Of course," she said. "I'm glad you're staying."

"I figured as much," Jake said, looking at his best friend and ranger partner of two years. "After you got that letter."

By now they'd nearly reached the sheriff's office and he was out front, waiting for them.

"Knew it had to me you two," the sheriff said, as they rode up. "Been hearing things."

"Lot's of folks around her have been swindled out of their land. And I have proof that Holland was the one who did it," Matt told the sheriff as they pulled up in front of the sheriffs office. "He killed my father for our land."

"Looks like you're the ones with the bodies," the sheriff said.

"I'll leave them with you, for the undertaker, if that suits you," Matt said. "Have a couple folks need doctoring."

The sheriff nodded. "That's fine," he said.

"Holland also kidnapped my sister," Matt said.

"You all right miss Truman?"

"Yes. I am now. I just want to get home to mama."

"She'll be worried." Matt said. "If we could get a message to her, we'd be much obliged."

"Of course," the sheriff said. "I'll send Will." He motioned to one of his deputies who'd come up to the building to see what was going on. "Will, ride on out to Mrs. Truman's place and let her know her daughter is safe and coming home."

"Yes, sir," Will said. He headed toward his horse and Carolyn gave a sigh of relief. "Tell her Matt and Jake are coming too," she called after him.

"Yes ma'am," he said, giving her a wide smile and a wink.

"Thank you," she smiled.

Jake turned to her and watched her reaction to the deputy, but didn't say anything.

It was several hours by the time the wounded had been doctored, the bodies were taken to the undertakers and each person had told the sheriff their version of what happened. Jose and Eli were now in jail and George and Bertha were spending the night with at the doctors. Finally,

Matt, Carolyn and Jake were riding back to the Truman ranch.

Matt looked at his watch. "Four hours to home," he said. "We'll be there before supper."

"It has been a long time," Carolyn said. "I'm ready to see mama and Dash and to sleep in my own bed." She laughed. "How much you want to bet mama makes a pie?"

"Do not take that bet, Jake, unless you're betting that she will."

"I take it your mama makes good pies?"

"Best in the county," Matt bragged.

"Then I hope she makes one," Jake said. "I do love a good slice of pie, with a glass of milk."

"Oh me too," Carolyn said. "Now you are making me hungry. Let's change the subject. Tell me about your rangering adventures while mama's not here to say no more talk about killing."

"I'd have thought you wouldn't want to hear that," Matt said. "Especially after what you've just been through."

"No I want to hear about your adventures," she said. "Tell me."

"Well there was that time we tracked Cobb Wilson," Matt said. "Time we found him he was dressed like a woman and trying to hide in a mining camp, acting like a washer woman. We caught up with him and he took off running. Pulling several lines of clothes down and drug them through the settlement, right through the mud. There was a picture of him in the paper after we shot him. Woman's dress and cap and all tangled up in string and shirts everywhere."

She giggled. "I can picture that. Tell me more."

The four hour ride home passed quickly as they told tales and she got to know her brother and Jake better. By the time they neared the ranch, Jake felt to her like an old friend. One she trusted with her life. Especially as he had just saved it.

She wasn't going to tell anyone but for the last couples hours she'd been thinking of ways to thank him and decided she really wanted to kiss him. Though mama might not approve. And she really didn't want anyone watching. She was going to find a way to do it. Even if it made her seem to bold. Watching his mustache and wondering if it would tickle was about to drive her crazy.

At one point Matt had asked her if there was anything she wanted to tell them or to tell just him before they got home to mama. Anything she needed to talk about.

"He was never going to let me go," she said. "I think he was crazy. He told me he'd wanted to marry me when I was still a little girl, but mama and papa said no. I don't even want to think of that. So I won't. But he also said my reputation was ruined now and if I didn't marry him, no man would. So I want to know what you both think."

"He's wrong," Jake said. He spoke so fast he made her head turn.

Carolyn looked to him.

"I would," he said. "And I wouldn't care about your reputation."

Eyes still wide, looking at Jake, she smiled. The smile lit her whole face.

"There's that smile I missed," Jake said. "I'm glad to see it's back."

She smiled even deeper.

"I will make it clear," Matt said, "That you, and your reputation are in tact. I'm not putting up with these rumors you've been telling me about. I'm going to make damn sure everyone around here knows us, and our family and we'll have no more of that gossip. You and mama deserve better than that."

"Thank you, Matt," she said. "Oh there's the split oak up ahead, we're almost home."

The oak, which had been split after a lightning storm but continued to grow strong, in two different directions, was one of her favorite landmarks. She beamed from ear to ear anticipating seeing the look on their mama's face when they came home.

Sally Truman was coming out of the barn, when she turned toward the riders. She shaded her eyes with her hand, peering to see.

Dash came out of the barn, barked once and then ran toward them at full speed across the yard to meet them.

"Carolyn!" Sally cried, as she turned and ran toward them, joy spreading across her face.

They slowed to a stop and then Jake slid Carolyn down to the ground so she could reach her dog and her mother.

"Oh, my baby. I'm so glad you're home safe again." Sally's eyes shone and her face was filled with the joy of seeing her youngest child again.

"Jake saved me," Carolyn said. "Him and Matt."

"Praise the Lord. You're all safe and home again. No one is hurt and no one is taking our land. I knew my Robert would never gamble our home away. He promised me I'd never be homeless again."

"We have clear title to this land and I'll be staying home to help you run the ranch," Matt said.

"Praise God for that," Sally said. "Now my prayers have been answered. Both of my children are home. We must throw a party. A barn dance, because Carolyn loves to dance."

"Oh, mama," Carolyn's eyes lit up. "I would love that! But isn't it too soon after papa's death?"

"No. And even if it is, I don't care. I thought I would lose you too." She shook her head. "No. When I tell everyone the reason, they will understand. You are home, and we are going to celebrate."

Carolyn listened to her and thought, *well if anyone can pull that off, mama can.*

She looked up at Jake, gazed into his eyes and asked, "Mr. Brace, do you dance?"

"Yes, I'll dance," he said. "But only if it's with you."

"Oh my," Carolyn's eyes widened. "I'll save every dance for you."

"Thank you," he said.

"Come on into the house," Sally said. "I've a fresh pot of soup on and there are pies in the oven for dessert."

"Pie!" Carolyn clapped her hands and turned to Luke. "See? We told you she'd bake pies."

"I've missed your pies," Matt said with a grin. "Apple or pecan?"

"Why one of each of course," Sally said.

"Pecan is Matt's favorite and apple is mine," Carolyn explained to Jake. "What is yours?"

"I'm partial to apple," he said.

"Then I'm glad I'm made an apple pie," Sally said. "I want to thank you for bringing my daughter home."

"You're welcome Mrs. Truman," he said.

"I hope you can stay longer and visit with us," she said.

"Oh yes," Carolyn said, her eyes lighting at the thought. "Can you?"

"That could be arranged," he said.

"Good," Sally said. "Well, come on into the house."

"I'll just see to the horses," Jake said. "You all go on. I'll be in shortly."

"I want to hear everything," Sally said. "From each of you."

"I'll be in directly, after I help Jake with the horses," Carolyn said.

"There's no need," he said.

"Oh yes there is," she said. "I'm helping you, and that's that."

"Well, I guess it is then," he said.

When the others had gone into the house, and Carolyn and Jake were alone in the barn, she moved closer to him and licked her lips while sneaking glances at his.

He watched the way her tongue moved and the way she was looking at him.

Well, I be darned, he thought. *If she isn't angling for a kiss, I'll eat my hat.*

"I want to thank you again," she said. "I'm finally home thanks to you and to Matt."

"Nothing to thank me for, sweetheart," he said.

"Oh yes there is," she said, stepping closer, gazing up into his eyes.

She wants to be kissed.

He had no doubt, and with that confidence, he reached for her and pulled her close up against his chest as his arms wrapped around her.

Her lips parted and her arms went up around his neck.

He bent to kiss her, his lips descending until they met hers in a sweet brush, touching, tasting. She tasted sweet as honeysuckle and her lips were soft beneath his, her body soft beneath his hands, her breasts against his chest. Everything about her felt soft and perfect.

As she opened her mouth, he deepened the kiss,

keeping it slow, remembering she might not have been kissed like this before. Remembering all she'd just been through and wanting to be slow and tender with her.

Their tongues met, touching, dancing slow as they explored each other.

Both pulled away slow, coming up for air.

"I know we haven't known each other long," he said, "But I hope to stay on a while, to help your brother with the ranch and get to know you better. If you'd like that."

"Oh good," she said, with a smile. "Yes I would like that very much. Now will you please kiss me again?"

"Gladly," he said. "Any time you want as much as you want."

"How much? How often?" She looked at him with hopeful eyes."

"Every day and twice on Sundays." Then he bent down and kissed her long and deep, again.

Carolyn was so happy to be in his arms and loved his kissed so much that she hoped he would kiss her like this just as he promised. Every day and twice on Sundays. He was the most handsome and the most fearsome man she had ever met, and his kisses were the sweetest thing she had ever known.

They stayed in the barn for a very long time making out, before they went into the house.

Before they bowed their heads for a prayer before supper, Sally clasped her hands together. "God has truly blessed us," she said. "Through our trials he has brought this family together and Jake too." She reached for his hand. "You're like family now," she said. "I want you to consider this your home away from home. But you must promise me one thing."

"Yes ma'am. What is the thing?"

"You mustn't keep Carolyn out in that barn too long. Especially if you're tempted to do things best kept for the wedding night."

"Mama!" Carolyn gasped.

"Now, daughter," Sally said. "I see the way you two look at each other and your father isn't alive to speak to this young man. One of us needs to. I'm sure Jacob understands."

He laughed. "Yes, I understand. And I give you my word. Your daughter's virtue is safe with me. I'm here to protect her, not bring her harm, or grief."

"I'll be the safest girl in all of Texas," Carolyn said as she slipped her hand into Jake's warm firm hand. "With a Texas Ranger to protect me."

THE END

SAMPLE CHAPTER: GONE TO TEXAS: A DESPERATE JOURNEY: CHAPTER ONE

CHAPTER ONE

KANSAS, 1867

"Gone to Texas." Reverend James Miller read the letter Luke had left pinned to the front door. "'I told you I ain't no farmer. I'm taking Matthew. It's time he learned to be a man.'"

"He's lying," Sally gasped.

Luke had never taken an interest in the children.

"No, Sally, I'm afraid not. That's what the letter says."

Sally Wheeler's world spun as she sagged against the door.

Texas. So far away.

His words hit her.

No. It couldn't be. He'd taken Matthew.

Speechless, she looked at Reverend Miller.

"You've had a shock." Reverend Miller touched her arm, his gaze warm and kind. "And I know you're exhausted."

He couldn't begin to know how battered and worn she

felt. The note had swept away her last bit of strength, leaving her completely drained. Her mind couldn't quite grasp the news. Her husband and son gone? This couldn't be real.

She'd gone without sleep for two nights helping Mrs. Harper birth her first baby.

Reverend Miller had shown up the second night prepared to baptize and bury, but thankfully both mother and child had lived. Then the reverend had been kind enough to give Sally a ride home.

She'd known Luke would be angry with her for staying away so long, but this—this was nothing like what she'd expected.

"How could he? He knew the auction was today."

She stepped inside and glanced about the bare cabin where her mother's furniture had once stood.

His guns were gone from over the fireplace, her things were scattered about, and a kitchen chair lay broken on the floor.

"Sally, what happened here?"

The reverend's voice reminded her she wasn't alone. It pained her to have him see the way they'd lived, the evidence of her poverty so clear. She hadn't been raised to live like this. She frowned. "I don't know."

All she knew was that she had only a few hours to pack.

"I'd planned to come back for the auction," Reverend Miller said. "But I'll stay and help you pack your things."

"Thank you."

"Do you have any idea what you'll do?"

"No."

I've left everything up to Luke, and look where that has gotten me. I'll never make that mistake again.

"I thought Luke had a plan," Reverend Miller said.

Well, apparently he did, just not one that included his wife and daughter.

She kept her thoughts to herself.

"You and Carolyn can ride back with me to the parsonage, when the auction is over," he said. "And you can stay with us until you sort things out."

Yes, she had much to sort out. But she had to hurry.

"There isn't much time." She glanced down at her dress, stained from the birthing. "I need to change my dress."

"I'll check on Carolyn then."

Sally nodded and glanced out the doorway, to where her three-year-old daughter lay curled in peaceful slumber, on the seat of the wagon.

She hurried to change, while darting anxious glances at the floor.

Are my treasures safe?

Reaching under the mattress, she removed the long iron rod she'd hidden.

Most nights Luke had returned home late, with liquored breath and empty hands.

She wished she'd had the courage to use it on him.

Sally slid the iron rod under a floorboard, and wrenched, lifting the wooden board, until it cracked. From the exposed cavity, she retrieved the carved box her grandfather had made, and opened it.

Thank God the jewelry is still here.

She pulled out her Mama's silver locket, her Grandfather's engraved, silver pocket watch, and her Grandmother's black and gold brooch.

Luke had gone into a rage, when he'd thought she lost them.

Her fingers traced the brooch.

The only permanent things she owned were from her family.

Reverend Miller knocked on the doorframe, and she jumped.

"Sally, Carolyn just woke up." He stepped inside holding her daughter, who rubbed one small fist across her eye.

Sally hugged the jewelry to her chest. There was no time to hide it. "Promise you won't tell."

He put Carolyn down. "Sally, if you have enough to save the farm..." His voice trailed off as he rubbed his chin. "I don't suppose it matters, now that Luke is gone."

"You can't tell anyone. Not even Martha."

He paused, before answering. "You have my word." He turned away, and headed for the door. "Hide them. If anyone asks, I can honestly say I don't know where they are."

She held out her hand to Carolyn. "Come help me pack your things, sweetheart. We're staying with the Millers tonight."

"Where my new dolly lives?"

Sally had promised her a new rag doll after they moved. But she hadn't had time to make one.

"No, she lives in our new home. We're going for a visit."

Reverend Miller pushed a large trunk he'd found in the barn into the cabin. "I'll load it, when you're ready."

Sally opened the trunk, lifted the quilt, and felt for the coins sewn inside.

They were still there.

Luke hadn't known about them.

She'd almost told him, but one glance around the now bare room, where her mother's furniture had once stood, proved she had been smart not to.

Luke wasted money hand over fist, and sold anything of value. He wouldn't have used her treasures to save the farm.

Surrounded by family heirlooms, Sally felt more like her old self. The quilt she'd made with Mama for her hope chest lay on the bed. She ran her hand over the knots and stitches, touching part of Mama's apron, and Grandfather's plaid shirt. Here were the pieces of her family history stitched together.

"I understand how hard this must be," Reverend Miller said.

How could he even begin to understand?

"And I'm sorry that you've lost your home."

Not as sorry as Luke is going to be.

She bit back the retort.

This is all Luke's fault. He gambled away every dime. He took, and took, and took. But this time he isn't going to get away with it. Somehow I will get my son back.

Sally nodded to the reverend then glanced about the cabin.

Her children had been born here. Despite the misery, she'd had moments of joy.

She knew each crack in the wall like her own hand.

As she packed their things, she found herself straining to hear Matthew's voice, though she knew he wasn't there.

Only the wind whistled through cracks in the walls.

The front door hadn't closed properly. It swung and banged in the wind.

Swing. Bump. Bang.

Each time it slapped, she jumped.

Like a ghost town, the cabin showed only a shadow of its former self.

She walked to the flower garden Luke had made fun of, telling her she couldn't grow anything but scrawny brats for him to feed. Words that stung like the back of his hand. But he continued to share her bed, uncaring that she might conceive.

The garden had been the one thing she did for herself. Wild mint had taken over, but the sunflowers grew tall.

She gazed across the flat Kansas land that went on forever. Once she'd thought it spread clear to the blue skies of heaven.

Sally gathered sunflowers into her apron. Carolyn called them "sun babies," and rocked them in her arms. She would save the seeds so Carolyn wouldn't lose her sun babies.

***

The auctioneer arrived, and in the distance she saw the wagons. Most of the town would turn out. Not because they wanted to buy the place, but for the entertainment the auction provided. And the gossip.

Sally felt like she'd fallen through the dry cracks in the Kansas soil.

Her ears rang with the final pounding of the gavel as the auctioneer called out, "Sold!"

The small gray cabin that Luke had never whitewashed was someone else's problem now, and as the townsfolk said goodbye, Sally's face stiffened from holding a forced smile.

She'd endured the curious looks. And the whispers of the crowd, the speculation of why Luke wasn't there, and what the pastor was doing holding her elbow, while Carolyn stood holding onto her skirt.

The feeling she might faint had passed, though her knees still trembled with fatigue.

"Sally?"

Hearing the familiar voice took her by surprise. She turned.

"Ozzie Moss!"

He'd led the wagon train that took her family to Kansas eight years ago.

"It's been years," she said.

He'd come by after Matthew was born, but Luke had made it clear he wasn't welcome.

Luke didn't like anyone coming around.

Especially Ozzie.

The feeling was mutual. Ozzie had warned her not to marry Luke.

"I'm so glad you've come."

In spite of his rough trail-worn appearance, he looked wonderful. Though he smelled ripe, and looked as if he hadn't bathed in months, she hugged him like a long lost friend.

Unaccustomed to showing emotion, he patted her back awkwardly.

"I was bringin' a load through, an' heard about yer troubles. I come to see how ye was."

Relief flooded through her. Now she knew what to do. She would convince him to take her to Texas.

"Luke took Matthew, and I need you to help me find him."

Ozzie frowned as she told him of Luke's note. He shook his head. "I knew he weren't no good. Now why would ye want to go chasin' after him?"

"I'm not going after him. I'm going to get Matthew back."

"Well, I ain't goin' clear to Texas this time. My route ends 'bout halfway."

"Please, Moss."

"Trail rides is rough. More so fer a woman. An' Sally, ye got a young 'un to care for. It's a powerful lot to take on."

"Sally, and Carolyn, are welcome to stay at the parsonage, as long as they need," Reverend Miller said.

"Well, then, yer safe here with good folks to look after ye." Moss nodded. "Good to see ye, Sally." He glanced overhead. "I'd best get to town, an' find me a room afore the storm comes." He gestured to his mules. "An' they've waited long enough fer supper."

Reverend Miller hurried to lash down the oiled canvas over the buckboard wagon. "Ready, Sally? Martha will have dinner on."

"More than ready." Her stomach growled.

Wind lifted her skirt, as she climbed into the wagon, and large drops of rain pelted her face. The rain stung, but nothing like the sting of losing Matthew.

She didn't look back at her home as they rode away.

The farm was lost.

She couldn't work the land alone, and it had become obvious Luke would never put the effort into it. It had been their home, but she would never see it again. She didn't care to see it again. Not after all she'd lived through.

She only wanted to see Matthew. To hold him, muddy knees, rumpled hair and all. She closed her eyes, and pictured the light dusting of freckles across his nose, and his gap-toothed grin where he'd lost a tooth.

As she pictured his freckled face, and his serious expression, she thought of how he never laughed when Luke was near. She thought of the dark side of her husband, the side she'd seen glimpses of. She couldn't help but feel, Matthew wouldn't be safe with him.

Even when Luke meant well, he was reckless and self-involved.

Luke had stolen her son. She could no longer make excuses for him. She could no longer believe he meant well. She could no longer listen to his lies.

Amid the shock she'd felt, since hearing the note, her anger stirred. The anger she'd never dared to show Luke.

She would never forgive him for this. But she *would* get her son back. Before something worse happened.

Riding to the parsonage on the wagon's hard bench, Sally felt jolted to pieces.

Water collected in rows in the muddy fields, where the corn never grew.

Carolyn tugged at her skirt, saying. "Mama, I'm hungry."

"I know, sweetheart. We'll eat soon."

Reverend Miller stopped the wagon, in front of the parsonage, and helped them down. "Tell Martha I'll be in once I settle the horses."

Sally grasped Carolyn's hand, and led her daughter to the one story house, with the lace curtains.

"Now, be on your best behavior," she said.

"Yes, Mama."

Sally knocked on the door, and then cracked it and called in, "Martha?"

"Why, Sally, what a surprise," Martha answered.

"Come in."

Observing Martha's tidy chignon, Sally tucked the loose strands of hair from her long braid, behind her ear, and smoothed her faded dress.

"Come sit down," Martha said.

Sally eased into a chair, and Carolyn climbed onto her lap.

Martha sat beside her, and leaned forward. "Sally, dear, what's wrong?" The intensity in her eyes heightened the sharpness of her nose. "It's late for visiting. Why, it will be dark soon."

Reverend Miller entered. "Sally and Carolyn are staying with us for a while."

He held out his hand. "Come along, Carolyn, we'll go milk Bessie."

She slipped off of Sally's lap, and ran to join him, placing her hand in his.

Sally rolled one shoulder, then the other, to ease the tension there. Her spine creaked with each movement.

"Where's Matthew?" Martha asked.

"Gone." Sally glanced at her work-worn hands, so rough compared with Martha's. "To Texas."

"Texas?" Shock filled Martha's face.

"I came home from the Harpers, and Luke was gone. He took Matthew."

A sharp pain tore through her chest. She couldn't catch her breath. Saying the words aloud stabbed like a knife.

He'd taken her son.

"Mercy. And you had no idea?"

Sally took a deep breath. "He left a note."

"Oh, you poor dear. And you not being able to read."

The silence of the farmyard had been her first inkling something was wrong. Matthew should have run to meet her, once he heard the wagon.

And Luke met any man who rode onto their place with his rifle in his hand.

"So he left you here, to deal with the auction," Martha said.

"Yes." Sally pursed her lips, unwilling to say more.

"My biscuits." Martha stood and rushed into the kitchen.

Carolyn giggled as Reverend Miller carried her in.

He settled her in a chair, and Sally sat beside her.

Thank God I still have my daughter.

"Carolyn," he said. "Our heavenly father looks down upon us every night, and hears our prayers. Let's pray, shall we?"

Carolyn dropped her head, as she'd been taught.

While they prayed, Sally added a silent prayer. *Please, Lord, keep my son safe.*

"Mm, dinner smells heavenly," Reverend Miller said, as Martha flitted around him, like a moth to an oil lamp.

"It's a good thing I know how to prepare a chicken properly," she said. "Seeing as how your parishioners pay you with poultry."

Martha scurried about, winding Sally's already tight nerves, until she felt they'd snap.

As Carolyn devoured her food, Martha exchanged knowing glances with her husband.

Sally's face heated.

Carolyn ate as if she hadn't been fed in days.

"You can stay, as long as you need," Reverend Miller said.

"Thank you," Sally said.

Martha is lucky to have such a kind husband. If only I'd been half as lucky.

"Perhaps Luke will find work, and send for you," he said.

"No." She shook her head. "He won't."

"Men say things in anger they don't mean. You mustn't give up hope."

Men do things in anger too.

She touched her jaw, remembering, and shuddered.

I don't want him back. But I want my son. Luke had no right to take him.

Sally forced herself to swallow past the lump in her throat, and held back her tears.

She couldn't let herself fall apart.

After dinner, Martha showed her to the guest room, and then left her alone with her daughter.

As she wiped Carolyn's face, and combed her daughter's tangled hair, the nightly ritual calmed her unsteady hands.

Rain pinged on the tin roof.

A streak of lightning outside the window illuminated the yard, then thunder rumbled off in the distance.

For months they'd been without a drop. Now it poured.

Matthew could be out in this storm.

She had no way of knowing when they'd left, or how far they'd ridden.

Luke won't stop for Matthew's sake.

Carolyn sniffled.

Sally stroked her cheek, the way she had when she was a baby until the comforting motion lulled her daughter to sleep. She kissed her forehead, and then lay back in bed, to stare at the ceiling.

No one will tuck Matthew in tonight.

She squeezed her eyes closed, as the thought tore at her.

Luke was wrong. He had to know seven was too young to learn to be a man.

Only last week, Matthew had lost a tooth, and said another was "wiggly."

She had to be there when it came out. She couldn't bear to miss a moment of her children's lives.

Her life had gone from bad to worse, from the day she'd said, "I do."

Marrying Luke had been the biggest mistake of her life, but at least she had the children.

Just when she'd taught herself to bear one more burden, another was piled on. She only had so much strength.

How much more can I take?

The wind howled outside, as if echoing the loss within her soul. She wanted to stand on the front porch and scream.

But she forced the feeling down. Luke had taught her that.

Stay quiet. Don't show your emotions. Attract as little attention as possible.

Now, tonight, she was full of all the bubbling emotions she'd held back, for so long.

Rain pelted the roof.

Sally wrapped her arms around her stomach, and curled on her side, as tears she'd held back finally burst free.

She cried until, in exhaustion, she drifted off to sleep.

Matthew stood on a hill, calling for her.

Luke rode up, and lifted him onto his saddle.

"Come home," she called.

Just when Luke turned toward her, she woke with a start, to a crack of thunder.

Her dream left her with a deep sense of loss.

The rains still fell, and her dream washed away, like the topsoil on the Kansas prairie.

Yet the strong feeling lingered that Matthew was in danger.

***

The next day Reverend Miller drove them all to town for supplies. He lifted Carolyn down, and she ran onto the porch.

"Mr. Walls!"

The short, pear-shaped man, with ruddy cheeks, settled his hands on his rounded hips. "My, look how you've grown. What can I get you today?"

"Lemon drops!"

"Oho." He chuckled. "This sweet child needs some lemon."

Sally turned to Martha. "Could you watch her, while I run an errand?"

"Why certainly, Sally."

Sally hurried to the livery stable.

As she'd suspected, Ozzie was there with his mules. "Mornin', Sally," he said.

"Good morning," she said. "How soon are you planning to leave, Moss?"

"Once Tar gits shoed."

"Take us along," Sally said. "I'll be glad to pay you."

He snorted. "I don't need yer money, missy. Keep it to feed that young 'un."

"Moss, I'm going after Luke, and if you won't take me, I'm buying our stage tickets today."

He squinted at her. "I done tracked many a critter, but fellers is harder. Some fellers ain't never found."

"We'll find them, Moss. I'm going to get my boy back, if it's the last thing I do." She placed her hands on her hips. "With you, or without you, I'm going to Texas."

Moss muttered under his breath, "Changin' a woman's mind is harder than tyin' down a bobcat with a piece of string."

"I'm already packed."

"Course ye are," he shook his head. "Cain't let ye head off alone. I'll come by the parsonage fer ye. But be ready. I ain't waitin'."

"Thank you, Moss." She gave him a quick hug, which

made him turn red, and then she hurried back into the store.

Sally placed coins on the counter. "Carolyn needs shoes."

"I don't have her size, but I can order them," Mr. Wells said.

"No, there isn't time," she said. Carolyn pouted.

"Mercy, child. That lip will fall right off," Martha said. She turned to Sally. "What do you mean there's no time?"

"Ozzie is taking us to Texas."

"Mercy, do you think that's wise? And who is Ozzie?"

Sally didn't have time to explain. "We have to hurry, or he'll leave us behind. We'll need new dresses." She pointed to one in the window. "How about that one?"

Carolyn's eyes followed Sally's finger, and she lost her pout in a giggle. "Yellow, like my sun babies."

"I have another, just like it, in your size, Sally."

She had to be careful with the coins, but they needed warm clothes to travel. Carolyn could hardly travel in her worn flour-sack dress, and Sally hadn't owned a store bought dress, since marrying Luke. She nodded.

Mr. Walls tallied the purchases, and then tied them with string. "A man was here earlier, asking about Luke."

Sally froze.

"Who was he?" Martha asked. "What did he want?"

"He didn't say, but he's not from around these parts." Sally bit her lip.

Who is this stranger, and why is he looking for my husband?

Luke disappeared suddenly. What had he done?

The bell over the door jingled, as a customer entered.

Sally turned to look, as if drawn by a thread.

A tall ,shadowy figure of a man, scanned the room, his

gaze lighting on her. Gray-blue eyes pinned her to the floor, and she held her breath.

"I'll be with you, once I help these folks," Mr. Walls said.

The stranger broke his gaze, nodded once, and then walked to the corner, where he turned his back, to examine the rifles.

A shiver crawled up her spine, sending her nerves on edge.

Who is that man? Could he be the same stranger Mr. Walls said was looking for Luke?

Robert Truman focused his attention on the rifles, to take his mind off of the striking woman who stood holding the hand of a small girl at the counter. Her curly red-gold hair, and large blue eyes in a pale face, had drawn his attention, the minute he'd walked in.

He'd briefly forgotten why he'd entered the store.

"There you are." The shopkeeper handed her a package. "Sally, are you ready?" the other woman asked.

Sally clutched her purchases, and nodded, sending Rob a nervous glance, from beneath her lashes.

For a moment, Rob wondered if she was the same Sally the saloonkeeper had spoken of. But he'd said nothing about Luke having children, and the child showed no resemblance.

Sally smiled at the shopkeeper, and her smile lit up her whole face.

Rob pushed his thoughts aside.

No, she was much too pretty, and wholesome, to be mixed up with the likes of Luke Wheeler.

The shopkeeper hurried them out, while ignoring Rob.

Why hadn't the shopkeeper told me about Luke's wife?

Rob watched through the window, as a man lifted the

child into the wagon, and then helped the women up. Then the shopkeeper stood outside, waving good-bye.

What a friendly little town.

He frowned as the wagon drove down the street, and the shopkeeper stayed outside, avoiding him.

He stepped out onto the porch, and cleared his throat once. "You neglected to tell me about Luke's wife."

The shopkeeper blanched. "She doesn't need any trouble."

Anyone who took up with Luke had more than enough trouble, and that was a fact.

"You'll have to get your answers elsewhere."

"I already know where to find her." Rob fingered his holster, as he watched the man's eyes. "There's something you aren't telling me. Something you're foolishly gloating over."

The man swallowed hard.

"Out with it."

"The woman in the wagon," he took a nervous step back, "was Sally Wheeler."

Rob whipped his head around to spot the wagon in the distance.

He should have suspected something when the shopkeeper rushed them out the door.

With two steps, he was off the porch, and mounting his horse.

So she *was* Luke's wife.

He spurred his horse to a gallop.

Luke had an eye for pretty women, and he preferred redheads.

But Sally was more than just another pretty face. Something in her vulnerable blue eyes had called to him.

He shook the thought away.

A woman could blind a man. Make him forget what he came here for.

Luke's trail had led him here. He'd waited a long time for revenge, and no woman was going to get in his way.

Sally tucked her hair under her bonnet. She had felt the stranger's gaze on her back. A chill swept over her, and she shivered. Her fingers rubbed the brooch at her throat.

Winter will arrive soon.

She rode to the parsonage in silent worry, as Martha alternated between speculating about what the stranger might want, and trying to convince Sally that she was making a mistake going after her son.

When the wagon approached the parsonage, Sally saw a tall, darkly clad man, seated in the shadows of the porch steps.

Luke?

She caught her breath. Her heart leapt, and she immediately looked for Matthew.

But as the man rose in one fluid motion, her heart sank. He was taller than her husband, and Matthew was still missing.

She and the Millers climbed down from the wagon, and headed for the porch.

"Good evening!" Reverend Miller extended his hand. "Reverend James Miller."

An air of isolation shrouded the man wearing the long duster. He removed his hat, but ignored Reverend Miller's outstretched hand.

She gasped.

The man with gray-blue eyes from the store. He must have arrived when Martha insisted we stop to talk with a neighbor.

He barely nodded at Reverend Miller. "Robert Truman."

His voice was low and smooth, as he stepped closer, and it sent a shiver through her body.

"Sally Wheeler," he spoke with an edge to his voice, "I'd like a word with you, alone."

His gray-blue gaze pierced the distance between them, as if to pin her there.

"No." She backed away, one step at a time, sensing danger in the quiet man, who followed her every step.

His eyes bore into her, as if reaching for her secrets. "I insist."

His hand closed around her wrist, in a firm, warm grip. She froze at the shock of his touch.

Her senses came alive, as if lit by a spark, which ran through her entire body.

His eyes flared in surprise, even as his fingers tightened. He stood so close her breath hitched. She could count the freckles under his tanned skin, trace the slight lines across his forehead, and touch the rough bristles on his chin and jaw, above his upper lip. His lip gave a slight twitch, drawing her gaze even more.

She swallowed hard, and forced her eyes back up to meet his.

Every inch of her wanted to pull away and run, but his grip was too strong.

Unshaven and rough, he smelled of horses, sweat and leather. She crinkled her nose. He needed a bath and a shave. She took a slow breath to calm herself, but his scent filled her senses, making her aware of his masculinity.

"Anything you have to say to me, say it here," she said.

"Mr. Truman." Reverend Miller moved beside her, as if to protect her. "What do you want?"

He released her wrist, and answered, without taking his eyes off her. "I'm looking for Luke Wheeler."

His steady gaze made her knees tremble.

"I went out to his place, but it was deserted. The saloon-keeper said to talk to Sally."

His cold gray-blue eyes looked her up and down, with a cool appraisal that stunned her. Men just didn't look at women that way. His eyes shone like silver lightning, and the tiny hairs on the back of her neck tingled.

Under his beard, the planes of his face looked hard, as if he never smiled.

She flushed under his gaze.

Robert Truman appeared to be Luke's age.

Yet age was hard to judge in the West, where the land wore everything, and everyone down, before their time.

How did he know Luke?

"What do you want with him?" Reverend Miller asked.

Robert dusted off his hat. His gray-blue eyes became flat and unreadable as stone. "He owes me." He placed the hat back on, and finished with absolute authority. "I've come to collect."

Her spine tingled with each word. Her nagging misgivings for Luke flared.

What had he done?

Once Robert's hat was back on, Sally could no longer see his eyes under the hat brim. She could only see his straight nose, and firm jaw beneath the stubble.

His jaw moved.

She couldn't tell if he still watched her, but she had a feeling he did, and she didn't like it. She fingered her brooch as strange, disquieting thoughts raced through her mind.

Who is he? What debt does Luke owe him?

She wanted to ask, but the words froze in her throat.

"I'm afraid you're too late," Reverend Miller said. "Luke took off, and his place was auctioned." He nodded to Sally.

"This lady is his wife, and that's their daughter. So you see, you're not the only one who'd like to know where he is."

If possible, Robert's features hardened even more, and the look in his eyes, as he stared into hers, only made her more nervous.

He glanced at Carolyn, frowned slightly, then glanced back to Sally. "I'll be in town," he said. "If you hear from him."

"We know where to find you," Reverend Miller said. "Ladies." Robert tipped his hat.

The scent of campfires and horses followed him, as he walked past. He swung up on his horse in one swift movement, and didn't look back.

As she watched him ride away, Sally's anger toward Luke flamed into a raging fire.

What kind of danger had he placed Matthew in?

Whatever he was involved in, he'd drag Matthew right into the middle of it. There was no doubt in her mind.

Robert Truman is a dangerous man.

SAMPLE CHAPTER: DANGEROUS TIES: CHAPTER ONE

NEVADA 1860

Pain erased all sense of time.

Lillian didn't know how long she'd hung, her muscles exhausted from the strain, her mind full of warnings she was helpless to do anything about.

Her throat was raw from screaming before Grady had gagged her. Now the cloth gag stuck to her dry tongue.

She squinted through tired eyes at the pail of water sitting by the edge of the mineshaft. She could look right down into it, the water taunting her with how good it looked, how it would taste cool and refreshing as it slid over her tongue, down her throat.

It would soothe her throat if she could just reach it. But there was no hope of that.

They'd tied her up and left her to die of thirst. Lillian closed her eyes.

No, don't look at it. Don't think of it. Think of something else.

Pain shot from her broken right toe up her ankle and leg. The scent of burnt flesh still filled her nostrils.

He'd seared the brand across the top of her breast.

Memory lodged in her body where pain radiated along with heat, echoes of his laughter still ringing in her ears.

A single tear slipped out and ran down her cheek.

It hadn't mattered what he did to her or how relentless they were.

She still couldn't tell them where the money was. She couldn't tell because she didn't know. And no amount of torture could change that one fact.

Lillian squeezed her eyes tight and prayed her lie had bought enough time to get away. Though how she'd ever get out of this she didn't know.

She had to get away before he returned, angrier than ever because she'd lied.

Mr. Thomas Shelton, her former fiancé, was probably well to California by now, and rich as the cream Lillian used to pour into her tea every afternoon. He'd done more than abandon her along with the promises he'd made to her. He'd left her to face the anger of everyone in town who he had robbed.

Dear God, but she was thirsty. If she could only have a drop or two of water. Lillian kept her eyes closed so as to not look at the pail again.

Mr. Shelton, the president of Shelton Security Bank and a widower had finally asked for her hand in marriage after months of waiting.

She'd thought she'd close the dressmakers shop. Fact was, she wasn't making much money. It hadn't been going well.

The women living in town or in the outlying areas did their own sewing and except for a few bridal gowns and mending the saloon women's clothing, Lillian had made no other sales.

Nevada was nothing like New York, where a woman needed a new gown for an event or wanted one simply because it was the latest new fashion.

She'd been foolish to follow her cousin out west, even if he was her only living relative. Carl was nothing like the boy she'd grown up with. Letters could be so deceiving and she hadn't seen him since he was ten.

Yet he'd written to her, urging her to come out west after her parents died. Convinced her it was better to be with family. He'd promised to help her set up a dressmaker's shop now that she had to make a living. She'd always enjoyed sewing for herself and her ailing mother, and the dresses she made, had always brought compliments.

She'd also been drawn in by the adventure of moving west, so she'd left the town she'd spent her entire life in.

Carl had been nice enough at first, helping her set up shop, introducing townsfolk to her. But after the first few weeks, he spent all his time playing cards and running up debts in the saloon and the mercantile, then expected her to pay for them.

He seemed to have the idea that because he'd done this favor for her, she was indebted to him for life. It was a debt she could never repay.

Carl thought she owed him and he thought she had the money. Even her own cousin didn't believe her.

The pain in Lillian's shoulders from the pressure of her own weight pulling her down pushed away her thoughts. Her arms being stretched for so long made her jerk and flinch, though she knew it was futile to fight and she had barely any fight left. But she couldn't help pulling against the ropes even though it only made things worse.

Oh, what she'd give for someone to cut her down and a fast horse. She'd learn to ride, as if her life depended on it.

***

Nick's horse made her way carefully down the mountain, his pack horse following along behind.

He wasn't far from town, and looking forward to a warm bath to wash away the dust from the trip and then a good hot meal. Maybe if he were lucky there'd be a warm and willing woman too. He'd been a long time without a woman.

It was then he saw her.

Long golden hair, which caught the rays of the setting sun, lighting those tresses up like a flame. Red-gold hair swinging in a gust of wind.

What the hell?

He blinked twice to clear his head, in case he was seeing some fools gold of a dream.

But when he opened his eyes she was still there, bound by her wrists, suspended over a wide mine shaft; her bare feet tied together at the ankles and her long hair blowing in the wind.

Who had strung her up and why?

He pulled his rifle out and rode closer, his senses on alert. The area appeared to have been abandoned, but he knew you could never trust appearances.

The appaloosa lost her footing briefly and rocks rumbled down the mountain. He tensed, waiting for a sound or for the end of a rifle to appear, but all was silent and still.

He slowly rode closer. The only sounds on the mountain were the wind and the steadier footsteps of his horse.

By the time he reached the woman it was clear there was no one else about.

He swallowed hard, shifted in the saddle as his thoughts shifted.

Damn, she's beautiful.

The knots are all wrong. Whoever tied her was no cowboy. If she struggled those knots will only tighten more, hurting her worse.

His fist tightened around the reins.

That's no way to treat a woman.

Her long hair blew in the breeze again. He rode around to the other side.

He had yet to see her face.

She heard horses through her dizziness, through a haze of pain. The horses' hooves steadily clopped closer and closer, bringing God only knew what.

Her heart began to race.

Dear God, not them again. Please don't let it be them. Not again. I can't take much more. I don't want to die here, today.

The horses stopped and the only other sound was the wind.

She could feel eyes upon her. She didn't want to look, didn't want to open her eyes for fear of what she'd see.

But she forced herself to open them, fought the fear and the dizziness, and for one brief moment her gaze met his.

Long enough to see his eyes were like summer lightning, intense, and flashing with some dark emotion.

Then her world went black.

***

Nick frowned when he saw the brand upon her breast.

Her blouse was torn, ripped down the side, exposing pale creamy skin so fair it clearly had never seen the sun. Newly drawn, in the shape of a curving "S" the scorched and bloody "S" was an abomination upon her breast, her skin.

The violence of such brutal torture hit him in the gut,

taking him by surprise for he was not a soft man and he had seen much.

Who the hell had done this to her and why?

His gaze traveled up to the perfect oval of her face, eyelashes which rested against pale skin, golden hair trailing down unbound. Her pale cheeks streaked with tears.

They'd gagged her.

She made no sound because she couldn't.

He clenched his fists. He wanted to hunt down the son of a bitch who'd done this to her and exact justice. He wanted to cut her down and take away the pain.

Her lashes fluttered and she opened her eyes to look straight at him, her eyes widening in alarm and pain. Fear flashed in her green eyes for one brief moment, before she passed out completely limp.

"No. Damn it."

Rope burns marred her skin and the front of her skirt was ripped. Wind caught her skirt and it blew just enough for him to see the bruising on one leg.

He looked up at the rope, which was fraying above her bound wrists.

Wasn't gonna hold. Need to get her down. Now.

"Son of a bitch."

That rope breaks and she'll fall to her death.

He gathered his lasso, looped it around, and threw it once to test it.

One chance.

It might be all she had.

With a sure and practiced hand, he regrouped and tossed a second time, this time a smooth vertical loop swirling.

As soon as the top of the lasso hit the front of her knees, he angled it under her feet and up, tightening the lasso around her legs. He pulled the rope tight, held it taut, looped the rope around his saddle horn, and pulled on the reins, to signal his horse to backup. As a trained cow horse, she knew how to pull back gently on the rope.

Slowly he pulled her closer, watching each breakage of the rope suspending her, as her skirt slowly rode up her body.

He dismounted and gentled his horse, patting her on the neck, reassuring her. Then taking hold of the rope tied to the woman's ankles, he eased up the rope, before reaching one hand underneath her knees, and one hand behind the middle of her back, to hold her. He was poised to pull her toward him.

Suddenly the rope snapped.

Her sudden weight pulled her backwards as her body fell, the quick momentum nearly pulling him forward down into the mineshaft.

He yanked her closer, preventing the fall, both of them falling flat on the ground with a thump.

Damn that was close.

He closed his eyes for a brief moment and blew out a breath.

Whew.

She was dead weight on top of him, all softness and curves, her hair spilling over both of them.

Her body felt limp and soft.

He blew the silken strands that had fallen across his face away and inhaled her sweet scent.

The sweet intoxicating musk of her body overwhelmed. She was bare beneath her skirt.

He didn't like the thought of what that implied.

Damn. Nick swallowed hard.

She's hurt and she needs to be cared for.

He rolled her over, off of him, and onto the ground. Then he stood, looking down at her, and clenched his fists, fighting for control of his anger.

She was lucky to be alive.

Lucky he'd come in time.

What exactly had been done to her, before they suspended her over the mine, leaving her to her death?

He bent down next to her, watching the way her chest rose as she breathed, eying the brand again, as he pulled her bodice up to cover her.

Who was the son of a bitch who'd done this to her? And why?

It made him madder than hell.

He was angrier than he'd ever been in his life. And he didn't even know her name.

NOTE FROM THE AUTHOR

Thank you for taking the time to read *Deadly Adversaries*, my third western. If you enjoyed the story, please consider telling your friends and/or posting a review. Word of mouth is an author's best friend and much appreciated.

Deadly Adversaries is my third western, which continues the story of Matthew and Carolyn Truman, the children in *A Desperate Journey*, along with Jacob Brace, who is Nick and Lillian's son. Dangerous Ties is Lillian and Nick's story.

If you haven't yet read *A Desperate Journey*, that is the western story which started it all, and was my first novel.

Thank you for reading and reviewing! - Debra Parmley

ACKNOWLEDGMENTS

Thank you to my husband, Mike Parmley, for the hours of discussion of the plot of Deadly Adversaries, and for his intensive hours editing of this story. For cooking dinners, and for suggesting western movies, and going above and beyond, to make third book in the set possible.

Thanks to those who helped me learn about guns of the west, which are so important to any wild west story, as well as the gunfight scenes: I must thank Charles "Tazz" Welshans, Robert Arrow, and Aubrey Stephens.

Thank you to my cover artist Sheri L. McGathy for this beautiful cover. Thank you to my beta reader and friend, Jocie McCade, for the last minute beta read. Thank you to Susan Boles, my BFF for help with the blurb.

To my readers, a huge thank you, for your love and support.

I'd long wanted to write this third book, to pull together *A Desperate Journey*, and *Dangerous Ties* with this third book. It wasn't possible, when the books were at two different publishing houses. Ten years after the publication of *A Desperate Journey*, I am pleased to be able to release the set.

Thank you to all my readers who have patiently waited for that day. It is now here!

ABOUT THE AUTHOR

Author Debra Parmley believes "Every day we are alive is a beautiful day," and she likes to give her readers and her story people a story that ends happily.

An Air Force veteran's wife, Debra writes suspense, and military romantic suspense, contemporary romance, historical romance, urban fantasy romance, fairy tale romance, holiday romance, poetry, and memoir.

Debra married her high sweetheart, whom she asked out after a five-dollar bet. After living in five states with her husband and their two sons, and then living 23 years just outside Memphis, TN, she and her husband sold everything in 2020 and now live and travel the U.S. in their 43-foot motorhome.

Debra is an adventurous writer who has sold travel and has walked the plank of a pirate ship off the coast of Grand Cayman. She has gone swimming with dolphins in Moorea, French Polynesia, has escorted a bus full of people through Scotland, and has set foot in 13 countries. She climbs lighthouses because she is afraid of heights.

You can see read about her travels on her Beautiful Day Traveler blog. https://beautifuldaytraveler.wordpress.com/

As Debra Bishop, she writes fairy tales for all ages, fantasy, and children's books.

Visit www.debraparmley.com

ALSO BY DEBRA PARMLEY

Military Romantic Suspense:

Green Brotherhood SEAL Team XII:

Finding Bryce, book one - eBook, paperback

Real Movie Hero, book two - eBook, paperback

Saving the Bellydancer, book three - eBook, paperback

Green Brotherhood Trilogy #1 - ebook box set, paperback

Brotherhood Protectors series:

Montana Marine - eBook, paperback

Defensive Instructor - eBook, paperback

Marine Protector - eBook, paperback

Marine Protectors box set - ebook

Blind Trust - eBook, paperback

A Triple C Ranch Christmas Wedding - eBook, paperback

Montana Delta Rescue - eBook, paperback

Montana SEAL Protector - eBook, paperback

Montana Rodeo Protector - eBook, paperback – 2024

Montana White Horse Wedding - eBook, paperback - 2024

Bobbins Sisters Trilogy:

Check Out – book one, eBook, paperback, audiobook

Check In – book two, eBook, paperback

Check Mate – book three, 2024

Single Title:

Aboard the Wishing Star - eBook, paperback, audiobook

Jenna's Christmas Wish - eBook, paperback

Western Historical Romance:

Gone to Texas: A Desperate Journey - (original sweeter version) - Large Print Hardcover, eBook, paperback

Dangerous Ties - eBook, paperback, audiobook

Deadly Adversaries - eBook, paperback

Desperate, Dangerous, Deadly: A Western Collection – eBook box set

Isabella, Bride of Ohio: American Mail Order Bride – (original sweeter version) - Large Print Hardcover, eBook, paperback

Penny from Deadwood - 2024

1920's Romance:

Butterflies Fly Free series:

Trapping the Butterfly – book one, Large Print Hardcover, eBook, paperback, audiobook

Dancing Butterfly – book two, eBook, paperback

Exotic Butterfly – book three, 2024

Poetic Butterfly - book four, 2024

Fairy Tale Romance:

The Twelve Stitches of Christmas – (short story) – eBook

Futuristic/Dystopian Romance:

The Hunger Roads Trilogy:

Another Change of Scenery – 2024

Down a Back Road – 2024

Into the Convergence Zone – 2024

Urban Fantasy Romance:

Vague Directions - ebook, paperback - 2024

Poetry Anthology:

Twilight Dips – eBook, print

Nonfiction Memoir:

Anywhere But Here: Our First Year of Full-time RV Living on the Road - eBook, paperback - 2024

Out of Print:

Protecting Pippa

Split Screen Scream

Protecting Zarifah

Vague Directions – short story

A Desperate Journey

Isabella, Bride of Ohio

Tales of Deadwood - anthology

We Know the Truth, Do You? Area 51 – anthology (going to the moon/time capsule)

Wounded Heroes - anthology

Hansel & Gretel: Down the Rabbit Hole – anthology

More Monsters from Memphis – anthology

Writing as Debra Bishop:

YA Fantasy:

The Rolling House – YA time travel fantasy

Children's stories

The Purple Unicorn - 2024

Fairytales:

The Sweetest Day - fairytale Hansel and Gretel story, eBook, paperback

Fantasy:

Gatalop – 2024

Bellserie – 2024